Wet and D

"We have to ski past frozen waters—that must be the lake," Nancy said, remembering the clue. "Then we should follow the shore until we come to the stream."

"Watch out from behind!" George warned. Dede and her teammates were moving up.

"Out of the way, slowpokes!" Dede called.

"Oh, no, you don't. . . ." Ned poled faster along the lake's edge.

"We're almost at the stream!" George shouted.

"You mean, *we're* almost there!" Denise called.

Ned had forged a path closer to the stream. The ground sloped sharply down to the water.

"Faster, Ned!" George cried, poling with extra vigor. "We can't let them—"

She broke off in a gasp as her right boot suddenly pulled free of her ski. George flew sideways, tumbling down the snowy slope—straight toward the frigid water!

Nancy Drew
Mystery Stories

Available from MINSTREL Books

NANCY DREW® 163

THE CLUES CHALLENGE

CAROLYN KEENE

A
MINSTREL®
BOOK

Published by POCKET BOOKS
New York   London   Toronto   Sydney   Singapore

This book is a work of fiction. Names, characters, places and incidents are products of the author's imagination or are used fictitiously. Any resemblance to actual events or locales or persons living or dead is entirely coincidental.

A MINSTREL PAPERBACK *Original*

A Minstrel Book published by
POCKET BOOKS, a division of Simon & Schuster, Inc.
1230 Avenue of the Americas, New York, NY 10020

ISBN: 0-7434-0689-3

First Minstrel Books printing November 2001

10 9 8 7 6 5 4 3 2 1

For information regarding special discounts for bulk purchases, please contact Simon & Schuster Special Sales at 1-800-456-6798 or business@simonandschuster.com

Cover art by Frank Sofo

Printed in the U.S.A.

Contents

1

Winter Wonderland

"Don't you love all this snow!" George Fayne remarked as her friend Nancy Drew drove her blue Mustang beneath the stone arch that marked the entrance to Emerson College. "The campus looks like someone spread a fluffy white blanket over the whole place."

"You mean, a *blinding* white blanket." Nancy had been squinting into the bright afternoon sunlight all the way from River Heights. On the campus snow covered every roof and tree, and drifts reached as high as the first-floor windows of the brick and stone buildings. "It is beautiful, but I can hardly see a thing. Especially with the wind blowing all the new snow around."

"I love it!" George said. Her short brown curls danced around her face as she opened the passenger window and leaned out to catch a snowflake on her tongue. "Talk about perfect weather for the Big Chill Clues Challenge."

"I'll say." Nancy tossed her reddish blond hair over the shoulders of the blue cable-knit sweater she wore over her jeans. "It'll be great to see Ned. But I still can't believe I agreed to spend two days competing in an all-out, *outdoor* treasure hunt with sports nuts like Ned and you."

"You know you'll love it," George said. "Besides, we sports nuts need a clues maniac like you if we're going to win the Clues Challenge."

Ned Nickerson, Nancy's longtime boyfriend, was a student at Emerson. When he called to ask if she and George wanted to join the Clues Challenge team from his fraternity, they both had said yes right away.

"I know it'll be fun," Nancy agreed. "The three other sororities and frats competing are really athletic, and the clues are tough. You know it's a tradition to hide them in places that are practically impossible to get to."

"Didn't Ned say one of the clues last year was hidden at the bottom of an old well?" George asked as she rolled her window back up.

Nancy nodded. "Everyone had to cross-country ski five miles through the woods just to get there," she said, laughing. "Then they had to use climbing gear to get down to the clue. One guy actually got stuck and had to be rescued by Ned's team."

2

"Sounds like my kind of treasure hunt," George said, her brown eyes gleaming.

Nancy wasn't at all surprised to hear that. George was crazy about sports and the outdoors.

"It will be cool to actually compete in the challenge ourselves," Nancy admitted. "Usually Ned's whole frat wants to compete, but we were lucky that just about all of the guys were tied up this weekend."

"And that the Clues Challenge rules allow outsiders to compete," George added.

Nancy turned onto a side road that led to the west side of campus. Students were colorful splotches against the snow as they walked along paths that were still being shoveled. Up ahead was a cluster of colonial-style brick buildings. Even from a distance, Nancy spotted the green-and-white banner that bore the Greek letters of Ned's frat, Omega Chi Epsilon. As Nancy maneuvered around a snowplow and pulled up in front of the building, she saw snowballs flying and people darting in every direction.

"Snowball fight!" Nancy grabbed her red parka and got out, dodging a snowball that landed on the windshield with a splat.

"Think fast, Drew!" called a familiar voice.

Nancy turned to see Ned scoop a handful of snow from a heaping mountain piled in front of the frat. Ned's cheeks were bright red, and snow was matted in his brown hair and all over his green parka and jeans. He let the snowball fly, a huge grin on his face.

"Hey!" Nancy jumped to the left, and the snowball caught only her sleeve. "This means war!" she yelled back, yanking on her parka, then reaching for a handful of snow.

She barely had time to crunch the snow into a ball before Ned reached her and buried her in a snowy hug.

"I'm glad you could come," he said, burying his face in her hair.

Nancy leaned back to grin up at her boyfriend. "Me, too," she said.

She jumped as another snowball caught her in the middle of her back. A hailstorm of snow, shrieks, and laughter came at her and Ned from all corners of the Omega Chi Epsilon yard.

"Um, guys?" George said as two more snowballs were lobbed from a corner of the frat. "In case you haven't noticed, we're in the middle of a war zone."

"Truce!" Ned shouted. He pulled off his scarf and waved it like a flag.

Half a dozen guys and girls tumbled out from behind trees, cars, and snowdrifts. Nancy waved hello to Grant Dempsey, a guy with short brown hair and a round face. She and George knew him from previous trips to Emerson. Most of the other faces were unfamiliar.

"Nancy, George, this is C. J. Thompson," Ned said as a guy with tousled black hair and blue eyes came up. "He's an Omega pledge, and—"

4

"C. J. Thompson?" George repeated, gaping at him. "*The* C. J. Thompson? The cross-country skier who broke the world record in the twelve thousand meters last year?"

C.J. gave an embarrassed laugh. "I guess you've heard of me," he said. Shaking the snow from his gloves, he held out his hand.

"C.J. is our secret weapon in this year's Clues Challenge," Ned went on. "I figure someone who's headed for the Olympics will definitcly give the Omegas an edge in the Clues Challenge."

"You guys will need all the help you can get," said one of the girls. She was a few inches shorter than Nancy's five feet seven inches, with high cheekbones, black hair down to her shoulders, and the most infectious smile Nancy had ever seen. "We Kappas are going to pulverize you guys," she said.

Nancy detected a challenge in the girl's dark eyes. There was also a special sparkle when she looked at C.J.

"This is Dede Mallone, my girlfriend," C.J. said to Nancy and George.

Ah, thought Nancy. That explains the sparkle. The three girls with Dede introduced themselves as Krista, Rosie, and Denise. All four were members of the Kappa Rho sorority.

"Nice to meet you," Nancy said. "Let me guess. Kappa Rho is competing against the Omegas in the Clues Challenge?"

"You got it," Grant told her. "The four teams that always compete in the challenge are from Omega Chi Epsilon, Kappa Rho, Sigma Pi, and Delta Tau."

"Which means that for the next two days, you and I are enemies," Dede said, giving C.J. a playful punch on the arm.

"Speaking of the enemy . . ." Ned said under his breath.

He nodded toward a girl who was just passing on the freshly shoveled path. Long blond hair fell over the collar of her red parka. She held a notebook in one hand and a bundle of blue-and-white fabric in the other. The expression on her face was serious.

"That's Joy Swenson, the president of Delta Tau," Ned said. "The Deltas won the Clues Challenge last year."

"Hey, Joy! I hope you Deltas are ready to say goodbye to the banner," Grant shouted to her.

Joy paused on the path and called back, "You wish." She shook out the blue-and-white fabric in her arms; the words Clues Challenge Champs were spelled out in bold white letters on a blue background.

"Take a good look. This is as close to the banner as you're going to get," Joy said.

"What is that?" Nancy whispered to Ned.

"The banner is the final prize of the treasure hunt," he explained. "The winning team gets to keep the banner until next year's challenge."

"I'm taking the banner over to SportsMania now

so Mr. Lorenzo can hide it along with the other clues," Joy said.

She whipped it back into a shapeless wad, which she balanced on top of her notebook.

"You've got your chemistry notes?" Dede said, gaping at Joy's notebook. "How can you even think about studying for a midterm with the Clues Challenge on?"

"As if I'd let anyone or anything stop me from winning," Joy said. "See you guys later."

George watched until Joy disappeared behind a snowdrift. "She sure seems confident," she commented.

"Joy is the kind of person who can be captain of the field hockey team, president of her sorority, and still ace every class she has," Grant said. "She's all business when it comes to the Clues Challenge."

"Who's Mr. Lorenzo?" Nancy asked.

"The owner of SportsMania, a sporting goods store," Ned told her.

"The company that used to sponsor the Clues Challenge went out of business, so Mr. Lorenzo agreed to take over," C.J. added. "He makes up the clues and judges the challenge."

"Sounds like someone we want on our good side," George commented, blowing warm air onto her hands.

C.J. laughed. "Unfortunately Mr. Lorenzo is totally impartial. But he's a nice guy. And his store is amazing."

"You and George can see for yourselves," Ned

said. "Our team still has to register for the Clues Challenge. Now that you two are here, we can head over there. We'll make a stop on the way to drop off your stuff at Centennial."

"Isn't that the dorm where we stayed last time we were here?" George asked.

Ned nodded. "My friend Penny and her roommate are away this weekend. They said you can stay in their room."

"Great," said Nancy, heading for her car.

SportsMania was housed in a spacious two-story building halfway down the main street. It was about a hundred years old, but the windows on both floors displayed skis, running gear, and basketball, football, and hockey equipment that were state of the art.

"Wow." George stepped through the entrance behind Nancy, Ned, C.J., and Grant. Her eyes flew from rack to rack, taking in the displays that radiated out from a circular counter at the center of the store. An industrial-looking metal staircase rose to an open loft area where mannequins modeled sports clothes. "I think I want everything!"

"Man, oh, man. I like the sound of that!" a deep voice spoke up from beyond a half-open door at the back of the store. Then a man emerged, closing the door behind him.

The man was about forty-five years old, with tinted glasses and brown hair pulled back in a ponytail. As he came toward them, Nancy saw that he was half a head taller than she was. Beneath the long-sleeved polo shirt he wore, she detected the solid, muscular build of someone who worked out.

He strode over to them with a grin and reached out to shake C.J.'s hand. "How's it going, C.J.? We just got some new telemark skis in. Care to take a look?"

The guy was a natural salesman, thought Nancy. Outgoing and very slick.

"I'm not buying anything today, Mr. Lorenzo," C.J. said apologetically. "We're here to register for the Clues Challenge."

"Right, right." Mr. Lorenzo led the way to the circular counter and slipped behind it through a narrow opening on one side. The blue-and-white Clues Challenge banner lay in a heap on the counter, next to a computer.

"Okay," Mr. Lorenzo said. He pushed aside the banner and tapped on the keyboard. "I just need to enter each person's name. . . ."

While he typed in the information, Nancy leaned across the counter and said, "George and I didn't bring cross-country skis. Ned said the equipment would be provided?"

"Absolutely," Mr. Lorenzo answered with an easy nod. "SportsMania furnishes all the equipment—on loan, of course. Everything you need will be in the lobby of the Emerson Sports Complex."

George glanced over her shoulder at the cross-country skis. "That's really generous, Mr. Lorenzo," she said.

"It's good advertising for the store," Mr. Lorenzo said. "Besides, I'm always glad to support a good athletic cause. And I came up with some great clues, if I do say so myself." He looked up from his computer long enough to arch a warning eyebrow. "You kids are in for the challenge of a lifetime."

"Bring it on," Ned said, grinning. "We're ready."

Mr. Lorenzo let out a deep laugh. "That's the spirit," he said, still typing. "As soon as I'm done here, I'll fit you for equipment and—"

He broke off and blinked in surprise at his computer screen. "Man, oh, man," he murmured.

"What is it?" Nancy asked. She leaned forward to get a look at the computer screen.

The entire middle of the screen was blocked out by a large black rectangle. Spirals of blue, green, yellow, and purple twisted around the perimeter. But what really got Nancy's attention were the words spelled out at the center of the rectangle:

YOU KNOW WHERE AND WHEN.
DON'T FORGET THE CLUES . . .
IF YOU KNOW WHAT'S GOOD FOR YOU.

2

Cyber-threat

"That message sounds like a threat!" Nancy said.

Ned and the others crowded around; they all looked shocked, but Mr. Lorenzo waved them back.

"No need to get all worked up," he said calmly. "People send all kinds of crazy messages over the Internet. See? This one is gone already."

Nancy looked again. Sure enough, all she saw was the list Mr. Lorenzo had typed.

"Maybe it was some kind of advertisement," Grant commented, glancing over Nancy's shoulder. "I get tons of that stuff on my e-mail. I just delete it."

"This wasn't like that," Nancy insisted. "Didn't you guys see it?"

George, Ned, Grant, and C.J. all shook their heads.

"Let me see if I can remember it." Nancy closed

her eyes, then nodded. " 'You know where and when,' " she said, repeating the words exactly. " 'Don't forget the clues . . . if you know what's good for you.' "

She popped her eyes open again and gazed expectantly at Mr. Lorenzo. "Whoever sent that must be talking about the Clues Challenge clues," she said. "Has someone been trying to intimidate you into handing over the answers?"

She thought she saw a glimmer of discomfort in the store owner's eyes, but then Mr. Lorenzo shrugged, and it was gone.

"You can't take it seriously," he said.

Maybe he was right, thought Nancy. But there was something else about the message that bothered her.

"Most junk mail is sent through e-mail," she said. "But this message wasn't. It appeared on your screen out of nowhere."

"How does someone do that?" C.J. asked.

"Don't ask me," George answered. "I'm no computer wiz."

"Whoever sent that message is," Nancy said. "Maybe we can . . ."

Just then the door to SportsMania was pushed open, and a man wearing a yellow parka hustled in. His eyes zeroed in on C.J., and Nancy got only a quick glimpse of his tanned face and white-blond hair before he lifted a camera and began snapping off photos.

"Excellent, excellent," he murmured, circling C.J. to get shots from different angles. "Just act natural. These are going to look great."

Nancy blinked into the blasts of light that flashed from the camera.

"You know this guy, C.J.?" she asked.

C.J. opened his mouth to answer. Before he could get a word out, Mr. Lorenzo stormed out from behind the counter.

"Hey, you can't barge into my store and harass customers," he snapped. His jaw clenched as he reached out, grabbed the man by the collar, and yanked him toward the door.

"I'm a reporter," the man objected, his camera banging against his chest as he tried to twist free. "I'm here on assignment. C.J., tell him!"

Mr. Lorenzo kept a firm grip on the man's collar. "You reporters are the lowest life-forms," Mr. Lorenzo muttered angrily.

The reporter blinked, straining against Mr. Lorenzo's insistent pushing. "What?"

"Mr. Lorenzo, stop." C.J. jumped forward, blocking the store owner's path to the door. "He's telling the truth. This is Randy Cohen. He's here to do an article on me for *Sports World.*"

Mr. Lorenzo took a few deep breaths, as if he were trying to calm down. At last he let go of the reporter's collar, but he continued to stare at Randy with an intensity that surprised Nancy.

13

That computer threat must have affected Mr. Lorenzo more than he let on, she thought.

"A profile in *Sports World?*" George said, arching an eyebrow at C.J. "I'm impressed."

Shaking himself, Randy smiled at George and said, "Once people read my article, C.J. will be the hottest athlete in winter sports."

"Awesome," Ned commented.

Randy checked his camera, then reached into his jacket pocket and pulled out a notebook and pen. "I'll be like C.J.'s shadow for the next few days while I get material for the article," he said.

"This won't get in the way of the Clues Challenge, will it?" C.J. asked.

"The treasure hunt you told me about?" Randy shook his head. "Trust me. You'll hardly know I'm there."

"I'm starved!" George commented a few hours later, her breath cloudy puffs in the cold night air as she headed into town. "You said the restaurant is close by, right, Ned?"

Ned wrapped his scarf around the collar of his parka, then pointed ahead. "This path comes out on the main street, up there where those lights are. The Eatery is one of the first places we'll come to. They have a big room in the back where we always have the pre-challenge dinner. C.J. and Grant said they'd meet us there."

"Just hearing you guys talk about dinner makes my stomach growl," Nancy said. "But I keep thinking . . ."

"About that message you saw on Mr. Lorenzo's computer?" Ned guessed.

Nancy nodded. "If someone *is* pressuring him to hand over the clues and answers, it must be one of the contestants. Someone who will be at dinner tonight."

"Or," George said as their boots crunched over the frozen ground, "maybe the threat wasn't serious, like Mr. Lorenzo said."

Nancy hoped George was right.

"Mmm. I smell pasta!" George sniffed appreciatively as she, Ned, and Nancy followed the maître d' through the main dining room. A hallway at the rear led past the kitchen door and an alcove with a pay phone and rest rooms into a spacious back room.

"Nice," Nancy said, glancing at the large round tables and the abstract paintings that hung on the walls. Almost every chair was filled, and the walls echoed with chatter and laughter. Nancy didn't see C.J., but Grant waved to them from across the room.

"You're just in time," Grant said, nodding toward two waiters who pushed through the kitchen door with platters of ravioli. "It looks like the first course is here."

"About time," said a guy who sat to the left of Grant. He had dark hair that curled over the collar of his corduroy shirt and a look of boredom in his big brown eyes. Grant introduced the guy as Dennis Garcia, from Sigma Pi. Two other Sigma frat broth-

15

ers, red-haired twins named Philip and Jake, were also at the table.

"Are you excited about the Clues Challenge?" George asked Dennis as she sat down next to him.

Dennis leaned back to make room for their waiter to plunk down a platter of ravioli and a pitcher of soda on the table. "Excited, no. It'll be a piece of cake compared to facing off against Midwest conference football teams," Dennis said, once the waiter left.

"I forgot to mention that Dennis is Emerson's top quarterback," Ned explained. "He *was*, anyway, before he injured his shoulder and had to be put on the disabled list."

Nancy didn't miss the cocky smile that spread across Dennis's face. He obviously was a lot less bored now that everyone was talking about how great he was.

"You're not afraid of reinjuring your shoulder in the Clues Challenge?" she asked him.

"I can handle it." Dennis's eyes were filled with confidence as he reached for the soda. "Like I said, the Clues Challenge is peanuts compared to what a quarterback faces when . . ."

All of a sudden he stopped talking, his eyes fixed on something behind Nancy. The room had gotten noisier, and when Nancy turned around she realized why.

"It's C.J. and Dede and their one-man press entourage," said Ned, who flicked a thumb at Randy Cohen. "Doesn't that guy ever put his camera down?"

Hoots and calls rang out from one of the other tables. Looking over, Nancy saw Dede's Kappa Rho sisters waving Dede and C.J. over. Randy sat down with them, pulled his notebook out, and started writing.

"Show-off," Dennis grumbled.

"Jealous?" Grant teased.

Apparently Dennis didn't see the humor. Glowering, he got to his feet and threw his napkin on the table. "I need some fresh air," he muttered.

"What's his problem?" George asked as Dennis disappeared down the hallway.

"Dennis has a thing about C.J.," Ned said. "Dennis and Dede went out on a few dates. But once she met C.J. . . ."

"I get the picture. Dennis hasn't forgiven C.J. for stealing his girlfriend," Nancy said.

"Or his top-jock status," Ned added.

The red-haired twins from Dennis's frat shrugged uncomfortably. "Dennis is a great athlete," said one of them. "But no reporter from *Sports World* ever wrote an article about him."

He leaned back as the red-faced waiter placed two platters of fried chicken in front of them.

"All I know is, the Clues Challenge is the biggest blast of the winter," Grant said, reaching for a couple of wings. "I'm not going to let Dennis wreck it for me."

"I'll second that!" George agreed.

For the next hour Nancy was too busy eating and talking to everyone about the Clues Challenge to think about Dennis. She and George met so many people, it was hard to keep them all straight. Nancy recalled meeting someone named Hanna from Joy's sorority, as well as another Sigma Pi frat brother—a guy named Malik, who had dark skin and braids.

People floated from table to table, and the room echoed with teasing challenges about who would win. By the time dinner was finished, Jake and Philip had migrated to the far side of the room, and Dede, C.J., and Randy had joined Nancy, George, Ned, and Grant at their table.

"Can I get some quiet, please?" Mel Lorenzo called. He had floated from table to table while everyone ate. Now, he stood next to Joy's table and tapped a glass with a spoon.

Nancy noticed Dennis behind him, at the end of the hallway to the main dining room. He was leaning against the brick wall, his arms crossed in front of his chest.

"I'll keep the motivational speech short," Mr. Lorenzo said. "I hope you all ate a lot, because you're going to need every ounce of muscle power and brain power you have during the next two days.

"Remember, the challenge runs from sunup to sundown tomorrow and Sunday," he went on. "We meet at the foot of the bell tower tomorrow morning at sunrise. I blow the whistle precisely at five-thirty. That's when you race for the first clue, at the top of the tower. Just to remind you, *all* the clues will be inside containers like this one."

He held up a plastic snowflake container about four inches in diameter. Its two plastic halves were hinged together.

Mr. Lorenzo put the container back on the table, then stepped to the side as the waiters came into the room with custardlike desserts.

"Man, oh, man. That looks good," Mr. Lorenzo said, eyeing the dessert. "Just a few more things. First, all searching for clues must be done outside. If there's a clue on a building . . ."

"Is there?" called out one of Dennis's teammates, the guy with braids who was named Malik.

Mr. Lorenzo shook his head. "You know I can't answer that. Like I said, *if* there's a clue on or near a building," he said, resuming his speech, "you have to get to it *without* going inside the building.

"Second, searching the campus for clues is off-limits from sundown till sunup. Any team that doesn't abide by that rule will be disqualified," Mr. Lorenzo went on. "Third, the Clues Challenge HQ is in the lobby of the Sports Complex. That's where I'll be with all the equipment. And last but not least . . . Good luck!"

Nancy clapped along with everyone else. "Mmm," she said as the waiter placed the serving bowl on their table. "That *does* look good. What is it?"

"Tiramisu," the waiter announced in an uninterested voice. "Italian cake soaked in espresso, with custard and powdered coffee on top."

As he passed out dessert plates, everyone grabbed one—except Randy. He hadn't even turned back to the table until the waiter plunked a plate down in front of him.

"I, uh, think I've got enough material for today," Randy said, reaching out to shake C.J.'s hand. "See you tomorrow morning at five-thirty."

C.J. waved and gave him the thumbs-up, but he seemed relieved to see the reporter go.

"It's good to get publicity," C.J. said. "But I'll be glad to have my privacy back after Randy's done with the article."

"He's a little pushy," Ned commented, grabbing the serving spoon for the tiramisu. He was about to dig into the dessert but paused with the spoon in midair. "What's that white powder mixed in with the coffee?" he asked. "Sugar?"

Nancy took a second look at the tiramisu, then frowned. "The coffee powder is dusted on in a perfectly even layer," she said. "But the white stuff is in clumpy little bits. It's like someone just dumped it on."

"Check it out," George said, leaning back in her chair to look at the next table. "*Their* tiramisu doesn't have white stuff on it."

"These look like bits of pills," Nancy said. "See the round edges on some of them." She looked for their waiter, but he was already halfway back to the kitchen. "Maybe we should ask someone in the kitchen about this," she said.

"I'll go with you." Ned grabbed the dessert, and he and Nancy followed the waiter.

As they entered the hallway, Nancy glanced into the alcove where the telephone and rest rooms were.

"Hey!" She stopped short, staring at some spots of white powder on the burgundy carpet beneath the pay phone. "Do you see what I see?"

Ned dropped to his knees and fingered the powdery bits. "It's just like the stuff on our tiramisu," he said. "But . . . what *is* it?"

"Hmm." Nancy's eyes flew around the alcove— until something on the small shelf beneath the phone caught her attention. "Pills!" she gasped.

There on the shelf were half a dozen white tablets. Some had been partially crushed into powdery bits that were identical to the ones on their dessert.

"Some kind of medication?" Ned guessed.

Nancy scooped the pills into her hand, frowning. "If it is," she said, "someone spiked our dessert."

3

Deadly Medicine

Nancy felt a knot twist deep in her stomach. "Someone wants to make us sick so we can't compete in the Clues Challenge," she said.

"But . . ." Ned blinked in confusion. "People from different teams were mixed up at all the tables," he said. "How could anyone make sure only people from another team would eat the spiked tiramisu?"

"Think about it," Nancy said. "No one was moving around when dessert was served. Almost every person at our table right then was . . ."

"From Omega Chi Epsilon," Ned finished. "Except Dede, of course."

Nancy nodded, closing her hand around the tablets. "That makes it pretty likely that whoever did this isn't a Kappa," she said.

She looked up as the kitchen door pushed open. Their waiter came into the hallway carrying a tray of coffee and mugs.

"Excuse me," Nancy said, walking up to him. "Could we talk to you for a minute?"

The waiter paused, his face red and sweaty. "This thing weighs a ton. Can you make it quick?" he said.

"Sure. Did you see anyone near the phone booth about the time you served dessert?" Nancy asked.

"Or maybe you saw someone in the kitchen?" Ned added. "A customer, someone who didn't belong there?"

The waiter let out an annoyed sigh. "They don't pay me to keep track of customers," he said. "I just serve food. Now, if you'll excuse me . . ."

"Wait!" Nancy angled in front of him, blocking his path. "If you'd only try to remember . . ."

"What is it with you people?" the waiter said, rolling his eyes. "Do I have a sign over my head that says bother the waiter? Customers have been tripping me up all night."

"I'm sure if you . . ." Nancy blinked as his words sank in. "Someone *else* talked to you?" she asked.

"I wouldn't say he *talked* to me. Practically bowled me over is more like it," the waiter corrected. "My tiramisu would have been all over the floor if the guy hadn't caught it."

"What guy? Can you tell me what he looked like?" Nancy asked. "Please . . . it's important."

The waiter stared at her blankly. "Sorry," he said, indicating he wasn't at all apologetic. Hoisting his tray higher, he pushed past Nancy into the back room.

"What a grump," Ned muttered.

Nancy barely heard him, she was so lost in thought. "Well, we don't know *who* spiked our dessert," she said. "But I'm pretty sure I know *how*."

"Whoever knocked into the waiter must have sprinkled the crushed tablets on top," Ned said. "That waiter's been serving our table all night. Anyone paying attention could figure out that he'd serve the dessert to us rather than to the other tables."

"Exactly." Grabbing her boyfriend by the arm, Nancy dragged him through the kitchen door. "We'd better make sure this gets thrown out," she said, nodding at the spiked dessert Ned still held. "And while we're at it, maybe we can get a plastic bag to put these pills in."

Ned nodded. "Not to mention a dessert that *hasn't* been spiked."

When they got back to their table a few minutes later, George, Grant, C.J., and Dede were all drinking coffee.

"You're back." C.J. grinned up at them as he stirred sugar into his coffee. "We were starting to think you decided to make a whole new dessert yourselves. What happened?"

His smile faded as Nancy and Ned told them

about the tablets. "Whoa!" C.J. glanced around the room in disbelief. "You're *sure* someone spiked our dessert? I mean, you still don't know what those pills are, right?"

"We can't be positive until someone identifies them," Nancy admitted.

"There's a twenty-four–hour pharmacy off Main Street," Ned put in. "We can go there tonight."

"And in the meantime . . ." Nancy thrummed her fingers on the table. "We have to think about who had the opportunity to—"

She broke off talking as her gaze landed on Dennis Garcia. Dennis, Philip, and Jake were sitting at the same table as Krista, Rosie, and some of the other girls from Kappa Rho.

"Hmm," Nancy murmured, half to herself. "Do you guys remember seeing Dennis standing in the hallway near the alcove?"

George turned, following Nancy's gaze. "Definitely," she said. "I saw him there while Mr. Lorenzo was talking. You think *he* spiked our food?"

Nancy started to answer, then stopped when she saw Dennis get up to walk out.

"I'm going to talk to him," she said. She jumped to her feet and caught up to him as he was pulling his black parka from the coatrack.

"Leaving so soon?" she asked.

Dennis shrugged. "Might as well head back to the frat and turn in," he said.

25

"I saw you standing over here before," Nancy commented. "I was wondering if you saw anything unusual when the dessert was being served."

"Such as?" Dennis asked.

Nancy held up the plastic bag containing the crushed tablets. "Someone put these pills on our dessert," she told him. "I think whoever did it was trying to make sure the Omega team won't be in peak shape."

Nancy watched Dennis's face closely. But if he was the one who had spiked their dessert, he showed no sign of it. He looked blankly at the pills.

"Give me a break," he said. "What is this, C.J.'s way of drumming up hot material for that *Sports World* article?"

"C.J. isn't like that," Nancy said. Turning the conversation back to Dennis, she asked, "Are you taking any medication for your shoulder injury?"

He angled a sharp look at her. "I don't need tricks to get the best of C. J. Thompson," he insisted. "When the Clues Challenge is over, there's going to be only one champion—me."

Nancy was going to remind him that it was a *team* competition. Dennis didn't stick around to listen, though. Zipping up his parka, he headed for the exit.

Hmm, thought Nancy. Dennis obviously thought of the Clues Challenge as a personal contest between himself and C.J. How far would he go to win?

❁   ❁   ❁

26

"So Dennis thinks we set up the whole crushed-pills incident just to spice up Randy's article about C.J.?" Grant said, after Nancy returned to the table and told them what had happened.

"That's ridiculous!" Dede said hotly. "But . . ." She turned to face C.J., her eyes flashing with uncertainty. "Shouldn't we tell Mr. Lorenzo what happened? If someone is trying to sabotage your team, he should know about it."

Glancing across the room, Nancy saw Mel Lorenzo. He was still at the table with Joy and some of the other Deltas. As Nancy watched, Joy, cool and confident as ever, leaned close and spoke into his ear. Mr. Lorenzo's expression changed. He shifted uneasily in his chair as Joy spoke to him, and kept checking his watch.

He doesn't seem like a super-smooth salesman *now*, thought Nancy.

"What could she be saying to him?" George said.

"I don't know, but Mr. Lorenzo doesn't seem happy about it," Nancy said.

The change in him was so curious that Nancy temporarily forgot her own reason for wanting to talk to him. She watched, puzzled, as Mr. Lorenzo squirmed in his chair. After a few moments he said something to Joy, gave a curt nod, and got up and left.

"Hmmm." Nancy frowned as her eyes jumped back to Joy. "Now *she's* leaving—by herself."

Ned sipped some coffee, looking over his cup at Joy. "You think she's up to something?" he asked.

"She sounds so confident that the Deltas are going to win the Clues Challenge," Nancy said, thinking out loud. "Maybe that's because she's doing something to make sure they win."

In that instant she made up her mind. "I'm going to follow her."

"I'll go with you," George said right away.

"Okay," Ned agreed. "Grant and I will take the pills to the pharmacy. We can all meet back at the frat."

"Do you see her?" George whispered to Nancy a few minutes later.

Nancy paused at the beginning of the snow-covered path that led back toward Emerson College. She and George had left the Eatery in time to see Joy turn onto the path. Now that they were at the path themselves, though, Nancy couldn't see Joy.

Globe street lamps stretched along the path, each surrounded by a pool of yellow light. "One of the lights is out," Nancy whispered back, staring into the blackness. "Maybe . . . Yes!"

A figure moved out of the shadows and back into the lighted part of the path. Nancy recognized Joy's blond hair and quick, purposeful stride at once. "That's her. Let's go!"

She and George kept about fifty feet behind Joy. For several minutes all Nancy could hear was the crunching of their boots on the snow. She didn't see

Mr. Lorenzo anywhere. Joy walked alone, carrying her backpack slung over one shoulder.

"Shouldn't Joy turn left up there to get to her sorority?" George whispered.

Up ahead, Nancy spotted the path that forked left to the West Campus. Nancy could see the lights of the sorority and fraternity houses. Joy had walked past the turnoff and continued toward the main campus.

"Maybe she's going to the Student Center," Nancy whispered, nodding toward an enormous, brightly lit building set at the edge of the lake. Plenty of other students were headed in that direction. Instead Joy veered right, down a side path that was lined on both sides with tall oaks.

"She's going to the Academic Quad?" George asked, gazing ahead at the brick buildings that rose out of the snow around a square courtyard. "At ten o'clock on the night before the Clues Challenge?" Even in the darkness George's doubt was clear.

She and Nancy picked up their pace. As they drew closer, Nancy could make out the gothic arches and corner turrets of the buildings. At one corner of the quad a bell tower loomed four stories high. A lantern outside the entrance of the tower illuminated a stone archway and stairs that circled upward along the inside wall.

"Hold it." Nancy grabbed George's arm as Joy stopped outside the arched doorway of the tower. "Quick! Duck out of sight."

She and George climbed over a snowdrift and crouched behind one of the oak trees. When Nancy peered around the trunk, she saw that Joy was still at the foot of the bell tower. She was checking in every direction before dropping her backpack to the ground, unzipping it, and reaching inside.

"What's she doing?" George wondered aloud.

Joy stopped suddenly, her head whipped toward the oak tree where Nancy and George were hiding. Nancy froze, thankful for the darkness and the winter wind that whistled through the trees. A moment later Joy bent back over her pack, rummaging inside it.

"The Clues Challenge starts right here in less than twelve hours," Nancy whispered. "If Joy is here now—"

She broke off as a faint noise from somewhere behind her and George caught her attention. She turned her head, listening carefully. After a moment she heard it again—the crunching of boots on snow.

"Someone *else* is coming," George hissed, whirling around. "Back there!"

It sounded as if the person was nearby, but they didn't see anyone. And the trees lining the path blocked much of their view.

"Come on!" Nancy mouthed, picking her way over the snow as quietly as she could. "I want to see—"

All of a sudden George let out a gasp, and Nancy turned in time to see George stumble forward. She fell against Nancy, sending both of them flying.

"I tripped on a rock!" George whispered, struggling to find her balance in the snow.

Nancy scrambled until she found her footing and pushed herself back to her feet. "Oh, no," she said, cocking her head to one side to listen.

The pounding sounds of boots on snow were faster now, and they were getting fainter and fainter. "The person's running away."

Nancy ran back down the path several yards, whipping her head left and right. "Where *are* you?" she said under her breath. But the footsteps had already faded. Between the darkness and the trees, Nancy didn't see anyone.

"Whoever it was is gone," she said, letting out a sigh. "I just hope Joy didn't hear. . . ."

"Too late for that," a voice spoke up right next to Nancy and George.

Joy stood on the path right next to them. Her hands were poised on the hips of her red parka, and her backpack was slung over one shoulder. In her eyes was an ice-cold glare that swept over Nancy and George like an arctic blast.

"Take some advice and quit following me," Joy said coolly. "If you don't, you'll be sorry."

4

You'll Be Sorry

Nancy faced Joy squarely. "I'm sorry if we scared you," Nancy said. "It's just that . . ." Now that she and George had been discovered, she decided to be direct. "We think someone may be trying to rig the Clues Challenge."

"You mean, cheat?" Joy's expression remained cool.

"Someone put some crushed pills on our dessert tonight," George said. "Plus, we're pretty sure someone sent Mr. Lorenzo a threatening message telling him to hand over the answers to the challenge."

Joy tightened her grip on her backpack strap and stared down her nose at Nancy and George. "What does that have to do with me?" she asked

"We're just trying to make sure the Clues Challenge gets off to a fair start," Nancy said. "We saw you talking to Mr. Lorenzo, and—"

"So you decided to follow me? How fair is that?" Joy snapped.

"You have to admit, this is a weird place to be, so late at night," George said, picking her way over the snow to join Nancy and Joy on the path. "Were you meeting someone?"

Joy pressed her mouth into a tight line. Her eyes flew over the snowy landscape, as if she were searching for answers in the night shadows. Finally she faced Nancy and George once more and said, "What I do is none of your business. Period."

Shooting one last glare at them, Joy turned and walked back down the path toward the West Campus.

George brushed the snow from her parka and jeans, staring after Joy. "Well, she's not going to win any Miss Congeniality awards."

"We obviously got in the way of something, and she didn't like it," Nancy said. "Too bad she heard us before we could figure out what it was."

As they headed back toward Ned's frat, they saw Joy ahead of them. Her silhouette moved farther and farther away, until it disappeared down the path to the West Campus. Just as Nancy and George were turning onto the path themselves, they spotted two familiar figures walking toward them from town.

"Ned! Grant!" Nancy waved, stopping to wait where the path forked off.

"We found out what the pills are," Ned said, holding up the plastic bag of white tablets. "Comptamine."

George stared at him blankly. "Run that by me again, only in English this time?" she asked.

"It's a muscle relaxant," Grant explained. "The pharmacist told us it's used to control pain and muscle spasms resulting from injuries."

"Say, shoulder injuries?" Nancy inquired. She slipped her hand into the crook of Ned's arm as they continued toward the West Campus.

Ned nodded. "Shoulder, neck, back . . . that kind of thing. The pharmacist says we're lucky no one ate the stuff. Comptamine has a tranquilizing effect, so it probably would have made us sluggish in the Clues Challenge."

"Wow," said Nancy. "So whoever put that stuff in our tiramisu really *was* trying to slow us down."

While they walked, Nancy and George told Ned and Grant about their runin with Joy. When they were done, Grant let out a whistle that echoed in the cold night air.

"Joy must have been meeting the other person you heard—the one who ran away," he said. "And I bet they were up to something underhanded. Why else would the other person run away like that?"

"Do you think she was meeting Dennis?" Ned asked.

"Maybe," Nancy said. "But why would he and Joy

34

meet on the sly? They're not even on the same team," she said. She blew out a cloud of breath, thinking. "Still, we should try to find out what medication Dennis took for his injury. And what he and Joy know about computers."

"Plus, we should tell Mr. Lorenzo about the pills," George added. "Maybe he'll tell us what Joy said to him that made him so uncomfortable."

"Most of all," Grant said, angling a warning glance at George, Nancy, and Ned, "we'd better watch our steps. Whoever spiked that dessert means business."

Nancy shivered involuntarily. She was glad to see the green-and-white banner that hung over the front door of Omega Chi Epsilon a minute later.

"I'll drive you and George back to Centennial," Ned offered.

He stomped over a pile of snow to the curb, where his sedan was parked. Nancy stayed where she was. She glanced down the row of fraternities, toward a guy who was headed up the front walk a few buildings down from Omega Chi Epsilon.

"Isn't that Dennis?" she said.

"Looks like him." Ned glanced up, then unlocked and opened the passenger door. "I guess he just got back from the Eatery."

Nancy went to the car, slipped in the front seat, and moved over to make room for George. "But Dennis left the restaurant an hour ago," she said.

"He told me he was going straight back to the frat to sleep."

"Hmm," George said. Her breath clouded up the windshield as she leaned forward to watch Dennis disappear inside Sigma Pi. "I guess he took a detour."

"Yeah. But where?" Nancy wondered. "And why did he lie about it?"

"Remind me why I volunteered to get up before it's even light out on a freezing cold Saturday morning?" George yawned, stomping her boots on the packed snow as she and Nancy walked toward the bell tower.

Nancy laughed. "What happened to being psyched about the ultimate physical challenge?" she asked.

"It's hard to get psyched about *anything* until I've had breakfast," George said. "Ned said he was going to bring us some, right?"

"Yup. Tea and muffins." Nancy eyed the ribbons of pale yellow light that began to brighten the horizon. "I hope he gets here soon. The Clues Challenge starts in less than twenty minutes."

Small groups tromped toward the bell tower. Some people were already there, stretching or jumping up and down to keep warm. Even in the dim light Nancy recognized a lot of faces from the night before. Like her and George, they all wore sleek warm-up gear and sweaters under their parkas. Only a few die-hard spectators, bundled up from head to toe, had braved the cold and the early hour to be there.

"Nancy! George!" Ned's voice rang out.

Nancy turned to see her boyfriend's tall silhouette walking up the snowy, tree-lined path with a thermos and insulated cups. Grant and C.J. were with him. All three guys wore bright yellow caps that glowed in the darkness.

"Omega Chi Epsilon!" Nancy said, reading the Greek symbols printed on the hats in neon green. "They're perfect."

"Tea *and* team hats." George grinned as C.J. pulled two more hats from his pocket and handed them to her and Nancy. "Okay. *Now* I'm psyched."

They were just digging into their muffins when Randy hustled up with his camera. "How about a team photo?" he asked. "Guys in back, girls in front."

C.J. had started toward Dede's team, which was doing stretches next to the tower, but Randy pulled him back. As Randy motioned for C.J. to take his place between Ned and Grant, Nancy noticed the team from Sigma Pi heading toward the tower.

Nancy didn't miss the way Dennis's eyes flitted between C.J. and Dede. Rolling his eyes at C.J., Dennis muttered loud enough for them all to hear, "We'll see who's the top jock around here *after* the competition."

"There's Mr. Lorenzo now," Ned said.

Mel Lorenzo was just walking up the tree-lined path to the bell tower, Nancy saw. His round face was almost completely obscured by his tinted glasses, knit cap, and thick scarf. His heavy ski jacket made his large frame look even bulkier than usual.

"Let's talk to him," Nancy said.

They caught up to him outside the arched stone doorway to the tower. "Ready for the challenge?" Mr. Lorenzo asked them.

"Ready, willing, and able," Ned assured him. "But before we start . . ."

He and Nancy told him about the muscle relaxant they had found on their dessert. As he listened, Mr. Lorenzo's expression grew more and more sober.

"This is a serious accusation." Mr. Lorenzo shook his head and gazed at them over the tops of his tinted glasses. "Man, oh, man. You say no one saw the person who . . . um, the person who . . . did it?"

Suddenly the store owner seemed distracted. His eyes were focused on something behind Nancy. When she turned, she saw Randy headed their way with his notebook open and ready.

"C.J. just told me about a possible sabotage incident," Randy said, tapping his pen against the page. "And what's this about threats to hand over clues? Care to comment, Mr. Lorenzo?"

"No," Mr. Lorenzo practically growled at the reporter, then walked away from him.

"Mr. Lorenzo," Nancy said, hustling after him with Ned. "We think whoever put those pills on our dessert could be the same person who sent you that computer threat."

"I already told you, that was nothing," Mr. Lorenzo insisted. His eyes kept jumping to Randy, who hovered nearby.

"We saw Joy talking to you last night. You seemed uncomfortable, and then suddenly you left," Ned said. "Did she say something that made you leave?"

Mr. Lorenzo held up a hand and shook his head. "I had to meet Jimmy, an employee. He hid the clues for me," he explained. "Joy was just making small talk."

He turned to Nancy and Ned with an understanding smile. "I'll keep my eyes open for trouble," he assured them. "But I'm afraid I can't suspend anyone from the challenge without much more solid evidence."

Nancy saw the doubt in his eyes. Mr. Lorenzo clearly thought she and Ned were blowing the whole thing out of proportion.

"Okay, everyone." Mr. Lorenzo pulled a whistle from his pocket and blew it. "To the starting line!"

Excited murmurs rose from all four teams. "This is it!" George said as she, Grant, and C.J. joined Nancy and Ned.

They had already agreed that C.J. would run for the first clue for their team. He took his place at the entrance, bouncing lightly on the balls of his feet. Joy, Dennis, and Dede's sorority sister Krista lined up next to him.

"On your marks!" Mr. Lorenzo called. "Get set . . ."

He blew the whistle, and all four runners sprinted

39

through the bell tower doorway. Shouts and cheers erupted from the crowd.

"Yes!" Nancy jumped up and down as C.J. took the lead on the stairs. "Go, C.J.! Go!"

The runners' pounding footsteps mixed with cries of encouragement from their teammates and spectators. The outer wall of the tower was dotted with small, diamond-shaped windows that rose in the same curve as the stone stairs inside. Nancy followed the flashes of movement as the runners sprinted higher and higher.

"They're almost at the top!" George said, squinting upward at the tower. "But I can't see which runner is—"

"Aiieeeeee!"

An earsplitting cry rang out from the top of the bell tower. The anguish—and pain—in the voice made Nancy shiver from head to toe.

"Oh, no," she said breathily. "Someone's hurt!"

5

A Cry for Help

"We've got to help!" Nancy cried. After shoving her tea into Ned's hands, she raced for the bell tower and pounded up the stone stairs two at a time.

Her heart thumped as she sprinted higher and higher. Surely she had to be near the top. As she raced past a window, she caught a diamond-shaped glimpse of branches and snow far below. And then . . .

"C.J.!" Nancy said as she stopped short.

He was doubled over on the stairs with the others around him, clutching his left ankle. "Owww," he groaned. "I think I sprained it."

"All of a sudden he slipped going up," Krista explained. "We plowed right into him."

"It happened so fast," Dennis added. "We were lucky we didn't *all* fall."

41

Nancy crouched down in front of C.J. "We have to get you downstairs—" She was interrupted as someone shoved her from behind. "Hey!"

Randy pushed past her with his camera, snapping photos. The blinding flashes made Nancy instinctively move up the stairs.

"C.J.!" Dede appeared below them on the stairs. Her face was red, and her eyes were wide. "You're hurt!"

She tried to get close to her boyfriend, but Randy blocked her way.

"Can't you get out of the way?" Nancy said. "Dede needs to— Whoa!" As she had moved up a step, Nancy's foot slipped out from under her, and she landed on her knees.

"Ow!" She winced, then did a double-take as she felt the surface of the step with her hand.

"It's slippery!" she said, rubbing her fingers together. "Someone rubbed this step with soap!"

"No way." C.J. whipped his head around—then scowled when Nancy showed him the soap marks on the step. "So someone tripped me up on purpose!"

Randy turned his camera toward the step. "Talk about great material," he said under his breath.

"Unless he's faking for publicity," Dennis muttered.

"C.J. would never do that!" Dede said hotly. She shot a furious look at Dennis. "How do we know it wasn't you? You'd do anything to get C.J. out of the competition."

Good point, Nancy thought and turned toward Dennis. At least, she tried to, but with everyone clustered around, she could barely wiggle.

"We need to get Randy to the infirmary!" she shouted above the din of everyone speaking at once. "He has to—"

"I've got it!" came a voice from farther up the tower.

Nancy turned around in time to see Joy trot down the stone stairs. She was clutching a slip of paper in her right hand.

"The first clue!" she crowed, holding up the paper. Joy shoved past Nancy and everyone else who had pushed up the stairs. "See you at the finish!"

Krista and Dennis looked at each other, then, carefully avoiding the soapy steps, sprinted to the top.

"The others can help me down," C.J. told Nancy. "Go get our clue!"

Nancy didn't have to be told twice. But as she ran up the curving tower stairs after Krista and Dennis, a troubling thought nagged at her.

How had Joy avoided the soapy step? How had she known to?

"I'm all taped up and ready to go," C.J. announced half an hour later.

Using a cane, he limped into the infirmary waiting room, his left ankle wrapped in an Ace bandage.

Nancy looked up from the slip of paper that

rested on the battered coffee table in the waiting room. She, George, Ned, and Grant had been going over their first clue while Randy observed from a chair.

"How is your ankle?" Ned asked.

C.J. shrugged. "It's a minor strain, nothing serious. This stuff is just a precaution, to keep from aggravating the injury," he said, pointing at the cane and bandage. "I have to steer clear of strenuous activity today, but if it feels okay, I'll be back in action tomorrow."

"Great," Randy said, raking his white-blond hair off his forehead. "That means we'll have time for some in-depth questions today."

"Speaking of questions . . ." Ned picked up the clue from the table and handed it to C.J. "Take a look at this."

As C.J. read the clue, Nancy glanced at it over his shoulder. Not that she needed to. She already knew it by heart:

> Shake it up at the start!
> Leave sculdiggery behind
> Lunge past frozen waters
> Run alongside the wet wanderer
> Bypass broken-down barriers
> Escape the bony clutches
> Navigate the trail to the ring of rocks
> Advance to the foundation of victory

Overturn the rising sun
Invite success!

"Looks like directions," C.J. said, sitting.

"Frozen waters must be the lake," Ned agreed. "But the rest of it . . ." He shook his head.

Grant opened up his backpack and pulled out a sheet of glossy paper. "Here's a map of the campus," he said, spreading it out on the table.

The lake was a blue oval at the center. A vast wooded section spread out to the west of it. Nancy followed a squiggly blue stream that threaded through the woods to the lake.

"Do you think that could be the 'wet wanderer'?" she wondered out loud.

"Could be," George said. "But it runs for miles. We need to figure out the rest of the clue first."

Nancy's eyes jumped to the top of the clue. " 'Shake it up at the start,' " she murmured.

"The start of what?" C.J. asked.

"I wonder . . ." Reaching into her own backpack, Nancy took out a pen and a small notebook. "What if he means the start of each line of the clue," she said. "The first letter from each line . . ."

She wrote down S L L R B E N A O I. "Okay. What if we scramble the letters?"

"You think *that*'s what Mr. Lorenzo means by 'Shake it up'?" Ned asked.

"Maybe. It can't hurt to try," Nancy said. She was

already spelling different words. *"Bells . . . beans . . .*
sail . . . rose . . . barn . . ."

"Wait a sec. There *is* a barn. The old Sanderford
place!" Grant jabbed a finger at the map, nearly
sending it flying off the table.

"That's right," Ned said. "The whole campus used
to be part of the farm. Woods have grown back over
the part of the land where the house and barn used
to be. I've never seen them, but from what I've
heard, they're wrecks now."

Nancy circled the *B, A, R,* and *N.* "That leaves *S,*
L, L, E, O, and *I,*" she said. "What did you say the
farmer's name was?"

"Sanderford," Grant said. "Ollie Sanderford."

"That's it!" Nancy crowed. "If you take the first letter from each line and rearrange them, they spell
Ollie's Barn!"

C.J.'s eyes lit up. He leaned on his cane to gaze at
the map. "Excellent! But . . . the house and barn
aren't marked on here," he said.

"That's where the directions come in." Nancy's
whole body tingled as she took the paper from C.J.
"We know the barn is somewhere in the woods. I say
we ski to the wooded side of the lake and see if we
can figure out the rest of the clue."

"I'll have to sit out this part of the challenge," C.J.
said. "Randy and I will meet you at the headquarters
later, okay?"

Ned jumped to his feet and grabbed his parka and

yellow team hat. "Mr. Lorenzo said he's got all the equipment in the atrium of the Sports Complex," he said. "Let's go."

The Sports Complex consisted of three modern, cubelike buildings that had been constructed at angles to the old brick gymnasium. Nestled between the buildings was a triangular, glassed-in atrium carpeted with AstroTurf.

"Ah!" Mr. Lorenzo glanced up from a table just inside the door to the atrium. He smiled as Ned sorted through the cross-country skis and poles stacked against the outer wall of the old gym, along with ropes, pins, harnesses, and climbing shoes. Everything was divided into four sections, one for each team. "I see the Omega team has solved the first clue. Good work. You're the second team out."

"Second?" George frowned at the blank spot beneath the Delta Tau sign. "Joy's team is ahead of us, huh?"

"Looks like the Sigmas and the Kappas are still puzzling over the clue," Nancy said, nodding to where the two groups sat hunched at tables on opposite sides of the fountain. Both teams watched as Nancy and the others put on their ski boots and grabbed skis and poles.

"Come on!" Grant urged, pushing back outside through the glass doors.

He, George, Ned, and Nancy stepped into their

skis. As they took off, they heard a loud whoop from inside the atrium.

"It's the Kappas," said George, glancing back over her shoulder.

Nancy felt a jolt of adrenaline as Dede and her teammates burst through the atrium doors with their skis. "Go!" Nancy urged.

She plunged her pole into the snow and skied forward. Beyond the parking lot, a corner of the snow-covered lake was visible. It was rimmed on one side by a thick woods of evergreens, maples, and oaks that stretched all the way to the horizon.

"This way," Ned called. He took the lead on a path that angled toward the woods.

"Hmm," Nancy said as her eyes fell on two buildings that had come into sight. To their left was a greenhouse, dominated by steamed-up windows and flashes of greenery. Just beyond it, to their right, the boathouse was nestled into the trees at the lake's edge.

"Hey, George!" Nancy called as she poled and glided forward. "Isn't sculling a way of rowing a boat?" she asked. "And isn't digging one of the main things that happens in a greenhouse?"

George looked back and forth between the two buildings. "Sculdiggery. It's perfect!" She whooped as they skied past both buildings. "We just left sculdiggery behind, guys! What's next?"

Nancy recalled the next part of the clue. "We have to ski past frozen waters—that must be the lake," she

48

said. "Then we should follow the shore until we come to the stream."

"The wet wanderer," Ned called back to them. "It'll take a while to get there."

As Nancy skied, she tilted her face up to catch the sun's rays. The wind whipped at her cheeks, but she was moving with such energy that she didn't feel the cold. She felt completely invigorated.

"Watch out from behind!" George warned.

Dede and her teammates were moving up, Nancy saw.

"Out of the way, slowpokes!" Dede called, grinning. She skied off the packed path, forging a new track that ran parallel to the one Nancy and her teammates were on.

"Pass 'em!" Rosie called from behind.

"Hey!" Nancy cried as Dede drew even.

"Oh, no, you don't. . . ." Breathless, Ned poled faster, and the Omegas pulled ahead again.

The two teams leapfrogged back and forth, skiing along the lake's edge. Nancy had never felt so exhilarated. Sunlight sparkled off one spot on the lake where there wasn't any snow.

"That must be where the stream comes in!" she realized. "The moving water kept that part of the lake from freezing."

Ahead of her George's head bobbed in a nod. "We're almost at the wet wanderer!"

"You mean, *we're* almost there!" Denise called as she skied parallel to Nancy.

Just ahead of them the stream angled off to the left. Ned and Dede had already veered away from the lake to ski beside the stream in parallel paths. Ned had forged a path closer to the stream. To his right, the ground sloped sharply down to the water.

"Faster, Ned!" George cried. She turned to glance at Denise, who had nearly caught up with her. George poled with extra vigor. She shot forward, angling around as the path curved next to the stream. "We can't let them—"

She broke off in a gasp as her right boot suddenly pulled free of her ski. George flew sideways, tumbling down the snowy slope.

"Help!" she cried, her arms and ski poles flailing.

"Oh, no!" Nancy's heart leaped into her throat as she watched George fly straight toward the frigid stream.

6

Cross-Country Catastrophe

"George!" Nancy's eyes flew left and right. She searched madly for some way to help George stop before she plunged into the icy water.

"The shrubs!" Nancy cried, jabbing her ski pole at the scraggly bushes that lined the stream. "Reach out and grab them!"

She didn't see how George could even see the bushes, she was tumbling so fast. All Nancy saw was a blur of poles, arms, legs. George's left ski popped off and skittered down toward the water. All at once George's arm shot out. Miraculously, her hand closed around some branches.

"Ooooh!" A muffled groan escaped George's mouth as she jerked to a stop. Her boots smashed through the thin ice at the stream's edge. George yanked them out instantly then sat up, dazed.

"Whoa" was all she said.

Nancy popped out of her skis and was next to George in a flash. "Are you okay?" she asked.

George got slowly to her feet, shaking snow off. "Nothing hurts. And the water didn't soak through to my feet," she said.

Nancy retrieved George's left ski, which was submerged halfway in the stream. After shaking off the water, she and George tromped back up to the trail, where Ned and Grant waited. Ned had picked up George's right ski and was examining it. Nancy saw Dede and the other Kappas behind the guys. They had all stopped and were watching George with worried eyes.

"Everything okay?" Rosie called over.

George didn't answer right away—she seemed to be preoccupied. "Skis shouldn't just pop off like that," she said.

"The binding popped off on one side," Ned said, turning the ski so George and Nancy could see.

Looking over George's shoulder, Nancy saw that one side of the binding had ripped totally free of the ski. A screw dangled from the screw hole in the binding. Nancy took one look at the blunt end of the screw and frowned.

"The tip's been sawed off!" she said, rubbing her finger against it.

George's whole face darkened as she stared at the screw. "You mean, someone sawed off the tip and then screwed it back into my ski?" she said.

Nancy nodded. "Leaving enough thread to hold the bindings on, but not enough to take the extra stress you put on the bindings when you skied all out."

Grant jabbed a ski pole into the snow. "Spiked food, soap on the tower stairs . . ."

"And now this." Ned shook his head in disgust.

Dede exchanged quick glances with her teammates. "I hope you don't think *we* had anything to do with these pranks," she said.

Nancy supposed any of the teams could be responsible—even the Kappas—but Dede had seemed genuinely shocked to see the soaped stair. Also, she had been sitting at their table the night before, which meant she could have eaten the spiked dessert along with the Omegas. Nancy had a hard time believing that Dede would do anything to harm her boyfriend or anyone on the Omega team.

"We'll consider everyone innocent until proven guilty," Nancy said.

"In that case"—Dede grinned at Nancy and skied forward—"see you at the clue!"

George watched with longing. "You guys go," she urged. "I'll meet you back at Clues Challenge headquarters."

"You're sure you'll be okay?" Grant asked.

"Go!" George insisted.

53

Nancy snapped her boots into her bindings and pushed off after Ned and Grant. "We'll meet you back at HQ as soon as we can," she said.

She didn't like leaving George, but she couldn't help getting caught up in the excitement as she spotted more of the landmarks in the clue. The "broken-down" barrier turned out to be a crumbling stone wall that had been part of the Sanderford farm. By following the wall, they came to an old family cemetery deep in the woods.

"That has to be the 'bony clutches' in the clue," Ned said as they skied past.

The Kappas were just ahead of them, but Nancy saw the Deltas beyond them, but skiing back toward them.

"The Deltas," Grant said.

Joy was in the lead, the wind ruffling her long, blond hair. Beneath her blue cap, her face was triumphant. She reached into her jacket pocket and pulled out a slip of paper.

"Looking for the snowflake with these inside?" she asked, waving the clue in the air. Without waiting for an answer, she shoved the paper back in her pocket and stepped off the path to angle around Ned, Grant, and Nancy. "We'll be on our way to the next snowflake before you get back to Clues Challenge HQ."

Joy skied on without looking back. The four girls with her grinned from ear to ear as they followed.

"You know . . ." Ned said once the Deltas were out

of earshot. "One of them could have sawed the end off that screw."

"Maybe. Or someone from Dennis's team could have done it," Nancy said. "But if they think this kind of stunt is going to stop us, they are *so* wrong."

Moments later they came to some snow-covered mounds that seemed to be the foundations of two buildings. The Kappas had stopped amid the stones and were walking around in their boots. There were footprints around both foundations.

"There's an old well," Grant said, pointing to a circular stone wall midway between the two foundations. "That must be the ring of rocks. But which is the foundation of victory?"

The stones of one foundation seemed to outline a larger space than the other. "I think the barn would have been bigger than the house," Nancy said.

Walking toward the larger foundation, she began to look over the stones. Then she spotted an iron weather vane—in the shape of a rising sun.

Nancy leaped forward and lifted one end of the weathervane. There, just below it in the snow, was a plastic snowflake identical to the one Mel Lorenzo had shown them at the pre-challenge dinner the night before.

Nancy opened the snowflake. Three identical slips of paper lay inside. Taking off her gloves, Nancy grabbed one clue and held it up. "Success," she whispered so the Kappas wouldn't know they had found their clue.

"Great," Ned whispered back. "Now let's rebury the clues and head back to Clues Challenge headquarters. We can find out if Mr. Lorenzo saw anyone messing with George's ski."

"Okay, let's take a look at this thing." Mel Lorenzo bent over George's ski, which lay in front of him on the table in the atrium. He could pull the screw out to check it closely through his tinted glasses.

"Well?" George prompted as she, Nancy, Grant, and Ned clustered around.

Finally Mr. Lorenzo put the screw down and sat back with a sigh. "The tip *might* have been sawed off," he said slowly. "But I can't be sure. The tip could have snapped off when the binding pulled loose."

Nancy gaped at him. Could he really be suggesting the ski hadn't been sabotaged? "Can you check the other screw?" she asked. "If the tip is missing from that one, too, we'll know someone sawed it off."

"Good idea," Grant said. "The end couldn't just break off inside the ski."

"Probably not," Mr. Lorenzo said. "But I don't think we should jump to conclusions before all the evidence is in."

Nancy exchanged surprised glances with George. Why was Mr. Lorenzo so reluctant to recognize the sabotage?

56

"Can you take out the other screw and check?" Nancy asked again.

Mr. Lorenzo shrugged and reached into a canvas bag that sat next to the table on the AstroTurf floor. "I threw some extra tools and supplies in here. Tape for the ski poles, extra hooks and pulleys, screwdriver, and file," he said as he sifted through the things. "I'm sure there was a screwdriver, but . . ."

"Did you say 'file'?" George said.

Mr. Lorenzo nodded. "I don't see it now, though. Or the screwdriver," he said. Letting the bag drop to the floor, he lifted the newspaper he'd been reading. "Where *are* they?" he murmured, scanning the table beneath.

"Isn't it obvious?" Ned spoke up. "Someone used your tools to sabotage George's skis."

Resting his elbows on the table, Mel Lorenzo pressed his fingers together in a steeple. "Show me the file and screwdriver in someone's pocket or backpack, and I'll be happy to disqualify that person from the Clues Challenge," he said. "But right now all we have is suspicion and . . ."

He frowned as Randy entered the atrium through a massive stone doorway that had once been the outside entrance to the old gym. C.J. was with him, using his cane to help take his weight off his bandaged foot.

"Not him," Mr. Lorenzo muttered.

"You're back!" C.J. swung over, an expectant smile

on his face. "You got the second clue?" His eyes lit up when he saw the slip of paper Nancy held up.

"As a bonus, I got a couple of mouthfuls of snow and an ice-cold foot bath," George said dryly. "Thanks to whoever sabotaged my skis."

"More sabotage?" Randy asked.

Nancy wasn't surprised to see him take the lens cap off his camera. "Did anyone check *your* skis, C.J.?" Randy asked.

Nancy felt a twinge of annoyance as he took a picture of George's ski, with C.J. bent over it. Everything was a story to Randy, even if it affected the welfare of their Clues Challenge team.

"Don't blow this out of proportion," Mr. Lorenzo warned, scowling at Randy. "Reporters get sued for printing lies, you know."

"That's why I need you to give me the facts," Randy said.

"Man, oh, man." Mel Lorenzo shook his head in disgust as Randy pulled his notebook out. "You'd better back off, pal."

Randy held up his hand. "Okay, okay. We'll skip the sabotage for the moment," he said. "How about giving me some background information for my article? C.J. says you just opened SportsMania a few months ago. Is the Clues Challenge your first affiliation with college sports?"

Nancy bit back a sigh of frustration. She wanted to ask Mr. Lorenzo if he'd seen anyone go through his

canvas bag. With Randy around, though, she couldn't get a word in.

"Forget it," Ned whispered to her. "We need to figure out our second clue."

"Let's head over to the Student Center for lunch," Grant suggested. "I'm starved."

"Sounds good to me," C.J. agreed. "Want to come with us, Randy?"

Randy turned away from Mr. Lorenzo, whose scowl had deepened. "Hmm? Oh—go ahead without me," Randy said. "I'll meet up with you later."

The Student Center was a large, old-fashioned stone building near the lake that had once been the president's mansion. Nancy and the others entered through a high doorway with carved-oak doors that led into a fancy entrance hall two stories high. They made their way past pool tables and a TV lounge to a huge ballroom that had been converted to a cafeteria. Tables covered the tiled floor, and stairs rose up to metal platforms where there were more tables and chairs. Nancy liked the way the old wood paneling and stained-glass windows mixed with the industrial stairs and furniture.

"Okay," George said, once they were settled on one of the platforms with burgers, fries, nachos, and sodas piled on their table. "Let's see the clue."

Nancy pushed aside her fries, flattened the piece of paper on the table, and read:

Baseball Is for the Birds (Are Your Ears Ringing?)

Needlenose on First
Flying Colors on Second
North Point on Third
Snowflake at Home

High fly towers over to score.
Ground ball doesn't make it.

"Huh?" Grant shoved a nacho into his mouth, then licked the cheese off his fingers. "I'm clueless."

Nancy read the clue from beginning to end a second time. "Well, we know it has to do with baseball. And it sounds like the snowflake with the next clue in it is at home base," she said, thinking out loud.

"Emerson doesn't have a baseball field," Ned said.

"What about those other hints? Needlenose, Flying Colors, and North Point on first, second, and third base." George took a bite of her hamburger, then washed it down with some soda. "Are there places on campus with those names?"

Grant took the map out of his backpack and put it on the table. While they ate, Nancy and the others pored over the map. But half an hour later they still hadn't solved the clue.

"We're missing something important," Nancy said, pushing aside her empty plate. "I mean, why does it

say 'Baseball Is for the Birds'?" And that part about a high fly scoring, but a ground ball not making it . . . Does anyone get that?"

When no one answered, Nancy got to her feet and pulled a hand through her reddish blond hair. "We need something to jumpstart our minds," she said. "Anyone want cocoa?"

Heads nodded all around the table.

"I'll come with you," George offered.

As they clomped down the metal stairs in their boots, Nancy spotted Dennis on the lower level in his black parka. He sauntered over to an empty table near the food counter. The red-haired twins, Jake and Philip, were with him, along with the two other guys from their team. Judging by their red cheeks and the way they rubbed their hands together, Nancy guessed they had just come in from outdoors.

"Looks like the Sigmas just got the clue from Ollie Sanderford's barn," she said, nodding in Dennis's direction.

She and George reached the main floor as the five guys plunked themselves down. Dennis zipped open a computer case, pulled out a sleek black laptop computer, and opened it. As Nancy and George circled behind their table toward the food counter, Nancy heard the computer whir and beep. She glanced at the wafer-thin screen and did a double take.

"Unbelievable," Nancy murmured, watching the intricate spirals of blue, green, yellow, and purple twist around the perimeter of Dennis's screen.

She grabbed George's arm, bending close to whisper in her ear. "Those are the same graphics I saw on the threat that was sent to Mr. Lorenzo's computer!"

7

Elusive Clues and Slippery Suspects

"What should we do?" George whispered back.

"I'm going to talk to him," Nancy said.

She was next to Dennis in three long strides. "Hi, guys," she said, keeping her voice as casual as she could. "Those are really cool graphics, Dennis. Did you program them yourself?"

Dennis's eyes jumped from Nancy to George, who was in line at the food counter a few yards away. His mouth curved up in a cocky smile as he asked, "Did your teammates send you here to spy on the competition?"

He hadn't answered her question, Nancy noticed. "I like your colorful spirals, that's all. Did you program them yourself?" she asked again.

One of the red-haired twins answered. Nancy

wasn't sure whether it was Jake or Philip. "The guy's a magician on the computer," he said, shrugging his parka onto his chair back as he nodded at Dennis.

That made Dennis the most likely person to have sent the threat to Mr. Lorenzo, but not the sabotage. Nancy knew she couldn't go back to Mr. Lorenzo without more concrete proof.

"One of George's bindings broke loose while we were skiing for the second clue," she said. She watched Dennis closely while she told him about the broken tip of the screw that had popped loose. "The funny thing is, the screwdriver and file were both missing from Mr. Lorenzo's tools," she finished.

"I'm sure Randy Cohen documented the whole dramatic event for his article," Dennis said. The sarcasm in his voice made Nancy bristle.

"You still think C.J. would sabotage the Challenge for publicity?" She waved a hand toward the platform where C.J., Ned, and Grant sat. "He sprained his own ankle!"

Dennis didn't bother to respond. "Where's C.J.'s shadow?" he asked as his eyes focused on the Omega table. "Maybe Randy figured out C.J. is all hot air."

Nancy ignored the jabs at C.J. "I noticed you got back to Sigma Pi pretty late last night," she said to Dennis. "Over an hour after you left the Eatery."

"Will you quit trying to prove I'm the bad guy?" Dennis said. "If I'm the one who's behind all this so-called sabotage, then why was our team the last to

64

find the second clue? I mean, wouldn't the idea be to make sure our team gets ahead?"

He had a point, Nancy thought. Still, there was something about the way he avoided her questions that bothered her.

Nancy's eyes fell on Dennis's computer bag. It lay unzipped on the floor next to his chair.

"Well, sorry to bother you," she said. "See you guys later."

As she turned away, Nancy made sure her boot caught on the strap of Dennis's computer bag. She tripped forward, and a jumble of things spilled from the bag.

"Sorry!" she fibbed, crouching down next to the bag. "I'll put it back."

She kept her eyes open for soap, or a file and screwdriver among the notebooks, pens, binoculars, gloves, and papers. Before she could touch a thing, though, Dennis had leaned over and scooped everything back into the bag.

"Now, if you don't mind, we've got a clue to work on," he said.

Nancy had no choice but to rejoin George at the food counter.

"So?" George asked.

"He's too slick to answer direct questions about the threat and sabotage," Nancy said. Her focus stayed on Dennis as she and George got hot chocolate and carried the tray up to their table.

"Too bad I can't keep this close an eye on Dennis all the time," she murmured. She placed the tray on their table, then glanced back over the railing at the Sigmas. "From up here we really have a good view of—"

She broke off suddenly and snapped her fingers. "That's it!"

Ned blew on his steaming cocoa, glancing curiously across the table at her. "*What's* it?" he asked.

"I get the clue—part of it, anyway. I think I know why baseball is for the birds," she said. "It's because we need to get a *bird's-eye* view before we can solve the clue. That's why a high fly scores!"

George nodded, taking a fresh look at the clue. "And a ground ball doesn't make it because you don't get the right perspective on the ground," she said.

"It makes sense," C.J. said. He pointed at the bottom of the paper. "Check out these parts about your ears ringing, and a high fly *towering* over to score."

"The bell tower!" they all said at once.

Nancy leaped to her feet, grabbing her parka and team hat. "Let's go!"

"Watch that step," Grant said as they made their way up the bell tower stairs fifteen minutes later. "It could still be slippery."

Nancy saw C.J.'s frown as he carefully planted his cane above the step that had been soaped. "I wish I knew who did that. . . ." he mumbled.

66

"We're working on it," Nancy assured him. "The important thing is that the sabotage isn't working. We still have a good chance of winning."

"Brrrr!" George shivered as they went into the circular room at the top of the bell tower. Wind whipped through openings in the stone wall, stirring the bells that hung from the stone ceiling.

"Wow. You can see the whole campus from here." George said as she stared through one of the openings.

"Not to mention the town," said Grant. After taking a pair of binoculars from his backpack, he looked out the other side of the tower. "Hmm. Isn't that Randy?"

Nancy borrowed the binoculars and spotted Randy, with his bright yellow parka and white-blond hair, just opening the door to SportsMania.

"It's him, all right." Nancy frowned, watching as Randy disappeared inside the store. "It's funny that he suddenly stopped sticking so close to you, C.J.," she commented. "I wonder what he's doing?"

"Um, guys? We're supposed to be finding the next clue, remember?" George said dryly. "Shouldn't we look for Needlenose on First, Flying Colors on Second, and North Point on Third?"

Shaking herself, Nancy joined Ned, George, and Grant on the other side of the tower.

"Look!" George pointed to a tall antenna at the top of the science center. "Do you think that could be the needlenose?"

"It looks more like a needle than anything *else* I see," Nancy said. "And if that's first base . . ."

She looked farther out over the campus, trying to spot something that could be flying colors. "The flag!" she crowed, pointing to the top of the Student Center. "It's in about the right place for second base."

Ned and Grant immediately turned to look for third base. "The North Chapel!" Ned cried, pointing to an ornate spire that rose up from a stone building near the dorms.

"So home base would have to be opposite the flag, and closer to us than the chapel spire or the antenna."

"The administration building?" George suggested.

The four-story brick building was down a small slope from the bell tower. Nancy lifted the binoculars to get a close-up view.

That was when she spotted Joy, in her red jacket, halfway up the side of the building. Her body was bent in a V, with her feet pressed flat against the bricks and her hands holding on to a drainpipe that rose vertically from the ground to the eaves of the building. Sunlight glinted off a plastic snowflake that hung from a window ledge just above her head.

"The next clue is there!" she said. "But so are the Deltas."

The Omega team got rock-climbing shoes, harnesses, and ropes from the Clues Challenge headquarters at the Sports Complex. By the time they got to the administration building, the Deltas were gone.

"Joy used the drainpipe to hoist herself up," Nancy said, letting her backpack drop to the snowy ground. "She wasn't wearing a harness or anything, but . . ." She stared up at the sheer brick facade of the building, broken only by windows. The snowflake, hanging from a third-story window, seemed impossibly high. Huge icicles hung from the eaves. Some of them almost as tall as she was. "It looks pretty dangerous."

"I can do it," Grant said. "I've done lots of rock climbing. As long as I have good traction, it'll be a piece of cake."

Nancy was glad to see that the gloves Grant pulled on had a rubberized palm. His climbing boots were flexible, with textured rubber soles that stretched around to cover the sides of his feet and toes. Taking a deep breath, Grant stepped onto the wall with one foot. It held firm against the bricks as he hoisted himself up on the drainpipe with his hands, angling his body out in a **V**.

"Good luck," George said.

Nancy watched silently, not wanting to do anything to break his concentration. She hardly dared breathe.

"Keep it up," C.J. murmured as Grant climbed slowly and steadily past the second-story windows. "You can . . ."

All of a sudden he frowned. "Did you guys see something move up on the roof?"

Nancy shaded her eyes with her hand. "Yes!" She gasped as something flashed above the eaves. It looked like an arm, but the sun made it hard to see clearly.

Crack!

"What—"

Nancy didn't have time to finish her question. A huge icicle broke free from the eave and plummeted right toward Grant's head.

8

Look Out!

Moving instinctively, Nancy grabbed her backpack and hurled it at the brick wall as high and as far as she could. Her eyes were locked on the deadly point of the icicle that was falling toward Grant's head.

With a thump the backpack slammed into the icicle, then ricocheted off the bricks and fell to the ground.

"Hey!" Grant flinched as chunks of ice rained down on him. His hands slipped on the drainpipe. For one awful moment his body swerved unsteadily. Nancy feared he would lose his grip altogether, but somehow he managed to get a steady grip with his hands and feet.

"Wh-what happened?" he asked, his face white.

George, Ned, and C.J. stood frozen in shock as

Nancy vaulted toward the main entrance of the administration building.

"Someone knocked that icicle off the roof," she called over her shoulder. "I'm going to find out who!"

"Wait up! I'm coming," Ned called.

They raced up the central staircase to the fourth floor. Nancy paused breathlessly at the top of the stairs. There was a seating area with plants and windows that overlooked the quad. The place was deserted.

Not surprising, Nancy thought. People wouldn't be working in the administration building on the weekend. Hallways led left and right, but she didn't see any way to the roof.

"This way!" Ned said, and led them past half a dozen doorways to a stairwell at the end of the hall.

"Footprints." Nancy pointed to wet boot prints on the stairs above them.

She pushed through a metal door to the roof and looked around. No one was in sight, but a trail of prints led through the deep snow to a raised parapet along the roof's edge and then back to the door.

Nancy hustled through the snow to the parapet and peered over the edge. Directly below her, she saw Grant had made his way down the wall to the ground.

At least he was safe.

"Hey, Nancy!" Ned called from behind her. "Look what I found."

She turned to see him bent over the snow a few

feet from the door. Ned straightened up, holding out a slender tool in his gloved hand.

"A file," Nancy breathed.

"And this," Ned added, holding up a green glove in his other hand. "Whoever was up here must have dropped them."

"Which means that whoever knocked the icicle off is the same person who filed the tip off the screw from George's binding." Nancy walked back over to him, took the file and glove, and put them in the pocket of her parka. "Come on. Maybe we can still find the person."

Ned and she made their way back down the stairs to the fourth floor. "Too bad the footprints have dried out," she said. "We'll have to guess which way the person went."

"There are three stairways," Ned said. "This one, the main stairs we used to get up to the fourth floor, and another stairway at the end of the other hall. I'll go this way."

"I'll take the main stairs. Meet you at the bottom!"

Nancy pulled open the door to the fourth-floor hallway. For a moment she stood there, watching and listening. Goose bumps popped out on her arms and legs. She was struck by the uneasy feeling that someone was there.

"Hello?" she said, but all she heard in reply was the sound of her own breathing.

Shaking herself once, Nancy moved quickly down

the hall. She tried each door she passed. Bursar's Office, Student Records, Financial Aid . . . They were all locked.

She was just about to start down the center stairs when a voice coming from the other hallway made her stop.

"I could have gotten in big trouble last night."

Nancy jerked her head around. I know that voice! she thought.

Hardly daring to breathe, she tiptoed down the hall toward the sound. Just beyond a rest room door was a bank of old-fashioned phone booths set into the wall. Three of the four booths were empty. But a half-open backpack and red parka spilled through the doorway of the fourth booth. As Nancy drew closer, she recognized Joy's blond hair. Joy's face was turned away from Nancy, but the tone of her voice was clearly annoyed.

"Okay, okay," Joy said into the receiver. "We'll meet again. But this time don't let me down."

In a single efficient motion, Joy slammed the receiver into its cradle and swung her arm around to scoop up her things. She was halfway out of the phone booth when she saw Nancy.

"Oh." She paused uncertainly. "I didn't know anyone was—"

Joy stopped talking and stared at the green glove that stuck out of Nancy's jacket pocket.

"Hey! Isn't that—"

She shoved her hands into her own jacket pockets,

74

then blinked in confusion when she pulled out only one glove.

"What are you doing with my other glove?" she demanded. Nancy was surprised by her accusing tone. Joy acted as if she was suspicious of Nancy, instead of the other way around.

"I found it on the roof," Nancy said. "Right after someone knocked an icicle from the eaves that nearly skewered Grant."

Joy blinked. "You don't think *I* . . . No way," she said, shaking her head firmly. "I haven't even been on the roof."

"Well, someone was. And you're the only one around." Nancy glanced up and down the deserted hallway. "What are you doing here all by yourself? Shouldn't you be with your team?"

Joy yanked the zipper of her backpack closed. "I don't have to put up with your third degree," she said, tugging on her parka and slipping her backpack over her shoulder. "And I won't stand for your making trouble for me."

"My team is the one being affected by the sabotage," Nancy pointed out. "C.J. hurt his ankle slipping on the soapy stair in the tower. George could have been injured when her ski was sabotaged. Who knows what would have happened if we'd eaten the dessert with that muscle relaxant on it . . ."

Joy watched impassively. "I didn't have anything to do with any of that," she said coolly.

"Oh, yeah?" Nancy countered. "Whoever knocked that icicle down dropped this." She held out the file Ned had found. "I think it was used to cut the screws on George's bindings."

Joy shrugged. "You've got a lot of nerve, trying to pin that on me," she said in a voice that was deadly serious. "I've had enough of your tricks. Back off!"

With that she strode past Nancy and started down the main stairs. All Nancy could do was stare after her.

"What is going on?" she murmured. Why was Joy acting as if *she* were the one being attacked?

By the time Nancy got back outside, Joy was gone. The sun was low, and the western sky glowed a deep purple-orange. Ned, C.J., and George surrounded Grant, who held up the paper clue.

"We're in business!" he said.

"Just in time." George cupped a hand to her ear as a loud air horn echoed through the air. "Hear that?"

"The signal to end the Clues Challenge for today," Ned said. "We'd better check in with Mr. Lorenzo at HQ," he said. "We don't want him to think we're looking for clues after hours."

Nancy's grip tightened around the file in her jacket parka. "There's something else I want to talk to him about, too."

When they got to the Sports Complex, they found Mel Lorenzo at the snack counter in the atrium.

"Excellent. You're the third team to check in," he said. He grinned at them as he picked up a can of diet soda and started back across the AstroTurf to the table where he'd been camped out all day. "I'm just waiting for the Sigmas now."

"While you're waiting . . ." Nancy pulled the file from her jacket pocket. "Is this yours?" she asked.

Mr. Lorenzo took the file and turned it over in his palm. "Could be. It's the right size. But I'm afraid they all look pretty much the same."

"We found it on the roof of the administration building," Ned said. "Right after someone knocked off an icicle that nearly killed Grant."

Mr. Lorenzo kept turning the file over in his hand as they told him about what had happened. He didn't look up or speak until after Nancy described her encounter with Joy.

"Wow," he finally said. Putting the file down on the table, he sipped from his can of diet soda. "Joy didn't mention the incident. You say she denied that she was the person you saw?"

Nancy nodded. "But we found her glove. Who else could it have been?"

"I understand what you're saying," Mr. Lorenzo said. "But without something more solid . . ."

"I know, I know. You can't disqualify her team." George crossed her arms over the front of her parka. "No offense, Mr. Lorenzo," she said. "But that really stinks."

77

"It's my job to judge this competition fairly," he told her. "I can't jump to conclusions."

Pulling Ned aside, Nancy whispered, "He's doing it again. Why does he keep going out of his way to try to convince us nothing funny is going on?"

"Maybe he just doesn't want any negative publicity," Ned suggested. "Bad press about the Clues Challenge could translate to bad business for his store."

"Maybe. But . . . I keep thinking about that computer threat," Nancy said. "What if whoever sent the threat actually convinced Mr. Lorenzo to hand over the answers?"

Ned shook his head. "It doesn't make sense," he told her. "If someone has the answers to the clues, they wouldn't need to sabotage us."

"True," Nancy agreed.

She and Ned returned to the rest of the group in time to hear Mr. Lorenzo say, "Just try to enjoy the rest of the challenge. You'll be at the Tropical Paradise dance party tonight?"

"Sure," C.J. answered. "Randy's going to cover all the Clues Challenge events, so he'll be there, too."

"If he ever gets back from his trip to SportsMania, that is," Grant put in.

Mr. Lorenzo's head jerked up. "Randy went to the store?" he asked. When C.J. nodded, Mr. Lorenzo blew out an angry breath. "Man, oh, man. Why can't that lowlife stay away from me?"

"Whoa," George said under her breath as they all

headed toward the glass doors. "I wonder why he hates Randy so much?"

"Add that to our list of unanswered questions," Nancy said. Shooting her friends a wry smile, she added, "The Clues Challenge is over for the day, but something tells me the mystery is just getting started."

9

After-Hours Sleuthing

The first stars were already twinkling in the evening sky above the lake when Nancy left the Sports Complex. All across the snow-covered campus, lights blinked on. Nancy stopped outside the glassed-in atrium just to look at the post card-perfect scene.

"Isn't that Randy?" she asked as a red Jeep pulled into the parking lot. Even in the darkening sky, his white-blond hair shone.

"Yup." C.J. waited until the Jeep stopped in front of them and Randy got out, then he walked over and said, "Hi. Where've you been?"

"Something came up," Randy said. He scooped up some papers from the passenger seat, folded them, and shoved them under the cover of his notebook.

He seemed distracted, Nancy noticed. His eyes

kept flitting toward the glassed-in atrium, where Mel Lorenzo sat.

"Is everything okay?" she asked.

"Um, fine," he said. "Just fine. Let's just—"

"Hey, C.J.!" a voice interrupted.

Looking over her shoulder, Nancy saw Dennis walking toward them. He stopped in front of C.J., his face red from the cold and his eyes filled with challenge.

"How about a race, C.J.?" Dennis said, shifting from boot to boot. "You and me. Right here. Right now."

"He can't race," George spoke up. "He's hurt."

"Oh, right. The big injury." Dennis's voice was heavy with sarcasm.

Nancy didn't miss the way his eyes flickered toward Randy. A satisfied smile slipped across Dennis's face as Randy reached for his camera and started snapping photos.

Is he doing this just to get attention, or to distract us from what's really going on? Nancy wondered.

"Hey, Garcia!" a voice called out.

Four silhouettes moved toward them across the snowy parking lot. As they came closer, Nancy recognized the rest of the Sigma Pi team.

"What happened to you?" Malik asked, stopping next to Dennis. "We waited two hours at the Student Center for you to come back. What's up?"

"I—" Dennis began.

"Save the excuses," Philip told him. "Let's check in

81

with Mr. Lorenzo so we can brainstorm the clue before tonight's party.

Dennis started to walk away, then stopped to jab a finger in C.J.'s direction. "Just remember, hotshot, I can show you up anytime, anywhere," he bragged.

C.J. just rolled his eyes. "Whatever," he said.

"Hmm," Nancy said as the guys from Sigma Pi went through the atrium door. "If Dennis wasn't with his teammates this afternoon . . ."

"Where was he?" Ned finished.

"The party doesn't start for another two hours," Nancy said. "There's something I want us to do first."

Ned turned to Randy, C.J., and Grant and said, "You guys go ahead. We'll meet you at the party."

George grinned at Nancy and said, "I know that look. What kind of plan are you cooking up, Nan?"

"It bothers me that Mr. Lorenzo keeps saying no one threatened him," Nancy said. "As long as he's still busy here . . ."

"You want to check out SportsMania?" Ned guessed.

Nancy nodded. "If we hurry, we can be in and out before Mr. Lorenzo leaves here."

Fifteen minutes later Ned, Nancy, and George paused just outside the patch of yellow the store lights shed on the sidewalk outside SportsMania.

"It looks like the place is empty, except for Jimmy," Ned said.

"Mr. Lorenzo's employee?" Nancy peered through the display window at the young man behind the counter. He was tall and gangly, with dark brown skin, black hair cut close to the scalp, and baggy clothes.

"You guys distract him," Nancy said. "I'll try to get inside Mr. Lorenzo's office and look around."

"Can I help you?" Jimmy asked as they came in.

George launched into a story about needing a warm-up suit. The young man led her and Ned up to the loft area. Nancy hung behind, looking at skis.

As soon as Jimmy was out of sight, she tiptoed to the office door at the back of the store, turned the knob, then frowned.

"Locked," she whispered as she pulled a credit card from her wallet. Quickly and carefully she worked the card against the lock.

"Yes!" she whispered as the lock clicked open. One quick step took her inside. Nancy shut the door quietly behind her and looked around.

A desk, some shelves, a copy machine, and a filing cabinet took up most of the space. It all had the same modern look as the rest of the store, but more cramped and messy. Papers and books cluttered the desktop.

Nancy began leafing through the papers on the desk. "Receipts, order forms, catalogs . . . Hmm. What's this?"

She plucked a thick computer printout from beneath some forms. At the top of each page, the words "Accounts Payable/Accounts Receivable" were printed.

Daily sales figures were listed, along with expenses for inventory, rent, insurance, and some payments labeled Miscellaneous. Nancy saw nothing suspicious, so she abandoned the printout and went through Mr. Lorenzo's desk drawers.

"Supplies, printer cartridges, business cards, more catalogs . . ." she murmured. Again, nothing suspicious.

"What now?" she wondered, sitting back in the desk chair.

At that moment Nancy's gaze fell on a trash bin that was tucked under the desk. It was a long shot, but . . .

Leaning forward, she began to pick through the crumpled napkins, old order forms, coffee containers, and discarded bits of paper.

Right under a Styrofoam dish still half full of fried rice was a crumpled piece of paper. After shaking a few greasy kernels from it, she smoothed the paper out on the desktop and read the words printed in capital letters:

MY PRICE JUST WENT UP TO $1,500.
PAY UP . . . OR I'LL TALK.

"Whoa!" Nancy's whole body jolted to attention. She looked at the note again, zeroing in on the amount. Fifteen hundred dollars. Hadn't she seen something for that amount in the accounts printout?

Nancy shot her right hand out and grabbed the printout. Her finger moved like lightning over the entries until she found the one she was looking for, near the end.

"Here!" she said under her breath.

It was a Miscellaneous payment for fifteen hundred dollars. And the date was . . .

"Yesterday!"

Nancy paged back through the printout. Exactly fourteen days earlier she found another Miscellaneous payment. This one was for one thousand dollars. And another thousand-dollar payment was listed fourteen days before that.

Flipping back, Nancy made note of every Miscellaneous payment in the printout. There were seven in all, made exactly two weeks apart. Each payment was for a thousand dollars except the last one.

"When the blackmailer's price went up," Nancy said quietly.

Her mind whirled at top speed. The note she had found made it pretty clear that Mr. Lorenzo *was* being blackmailed. But whoever had left that note wanted more than just the answers to the Clues Challenge.

Someone was blackmailing Mr. Lorenzo for serious money.

10

Blackmail

George and Ned were still in the loft of Sports Mania with Jimmy when Nancy found them again. She paused at the top of the metal stairs, watching while George modeled a bright red warm-up suit.

"I don't know about the color . . ." George said.

As soon as Nancy gave her a thumbs-up sign, George pulled the suit off and handed it back to Jimmy.

"I'll pass for now," she said, grabbing her parka and heading for the stairs.

Ned dumped another warm-up outfit into Jimmy's arms and followed George. They clattered down the stairs behind Nancy, leaving Jimmy alone in the loft area.

"You found something?" Ned said as soon as they were outside.

Nancy showed him and George the note and told them about the miscellaneous payments.

"So someone *is* blackmailing Mr. Lorenzo!" George wrapped her scarf around the collar of her parka as they made they way back toward campus. "But . . . is it the same person who's been sabotaging us?"

"That's the million-dollar question," Nancy said. "The payments go back to the beginning of October."

"I doubt those payments have anything to do with the Clues Challenge," Ned said, hunching against the wind. "Mr. Lorenzo didn't agree to sponsor the Clues Challenge until about three weeks ago. It was already November."

"On the other hand the last payoff was made just yesterday." Nancy shot a meaningful glance at her friends. "The same day Mr. Lorenzo received that computer threat."

"There could be a connection," George finished. "Dennis and Joy were both out on their own after the pre-challenge dinner. But"—she gave a shake of her head, as if she were trying to clear it—"why would either of them blackmail Mr. Lorenzo?"

The question hung in the air as they started through the woods toward campus. Wind whistled eerily through the tree branches.

"I'm starting to wonder about someone else, too,"

she said. "Have you guys noticed how Mr. Lorenzo reacts to Randy?" Nancy asked.

George chuckled. "You mean, like Randy is a plague that could destroy the human race?"

Ned shrugged. "That doesn't mean Randy is blackmailing him. Randy didn't even show up at Emerson until yesterday, and the blackmail started a lot longer ago than that."

Nancy sighed, trying to figure it out. "All I know is that Mr. Lorenzo overreacts whenever Randy is around—and I'd like to find out why," she said.

"Wow. This place looks great!" Nancy said, an hour and a half later.

She, George, and Ned paused in the doorway of the Attic, a large, open room at the top of the Student Center. A dozen dormer windows formed alcoves that were furnished with sofas, chairs, and coffee tables. At the far end of the room a band played on a low platform, and the dance floor was already packed.

"Check out the tropical decor." George bobbed her head to the music as she took in the beach scene that someone had painted on the walls in glowing, iridescent colors.

"Luckily, we're dressed to match!" said Nancy. She took off her parka, yellow team hat, and heavy sweater to reveal a flowered sarong skirt and tank top. George had on shorts and a tennis shirt, while Ned wore a red-and-white Hawaiian shirt with jeans.

An alcove right next to the door was fitted with hooks and shelves.

"Looks like C.J. and Grant are already here," Ned said, pointing to the bright yellow Omega team hats that lay on one of the shelves. He grinned at Nancy and George. "Let's dance!"

Nancy barely had time to hang up her stuff before Ned dragged her and George to the dance floor.

"After a day outside in the freezing cold, it feels good to work up a sweat," she said over the music.

C.J. and Dede were already dancing. And Grant left a soda on the counter to come over to dance with George. Nancy caught sight of most of the other Clues Challenge contestants, but it was so much fun to be close to Ned that Nancy didn't pay much attention to anyone but him.

"I need a break!" she said after six long songs.

While Ned headed to the counter for sodas, Nancy searched for a place to sit.

"That must be Randy," she murmured as the flash from a camera made her blink.

He was taking pictures of C.J. and Dede from an alcove near the dance floor. Seeing that the two other chairs in the alcove were empty, Nancy quickly wound through the crowd to him.

"Still working on your article?" she asked.

"That's what I'm here for." Randy snapped off another shot, then gestured to the empty chairs. "Have a seat."

"Thanks." As she sat down, Nancy glanced curiously at him. "Do you work in this area a lot?" she asked. If he did, then it was possible that he knew Mr. Lorenzo from before.

"I usually cover the West Coast," Randy told her. "This is my first time here. I'm out of film," he said. "I've got another roll in my jacket. Be back in a sec."

After he disappeared, Nancy noticed his notebook. It lay on the coffee table in front of them. Inside the front cover were the folded-up sheets from his Jeep that Nancy had seen him put there earlier. Right *after* he'd spent the afternoon away from Randy, she remembered.

Nancy glanced quickly over the crowd. Then taking a deep breath, she slipped the papers out and unfolded them.

"A fax," she murmured. The cover sheet showed that it had been sent to Randy at the Emerson Inn that afternoon.

Nancy flipped to the page beneath. It was a copy of a *Sports World* article, dated three years earlier. The title was, "Point-Fixing Scandal Ruins Western Tech." And the name on the byline was . . .

"Randy Cohen," Nancy murmured.

Why would Randy want an article he wrote three years earlier?

Quickly Nancy read on: "Three of Western Tech's top basketball players were expelled last week after admitting their involvement in a point-fixing scam."

Nancy knew it was illegal for players to score low on purpose to lose games. She also knew that there was lots of gambling on college basketball games and that point fixing was a way to guarantee winning big money.

What did that have to do with what was going on at the Clues Challenge?

Nancy turned her attention back to the article: "Ty Brubaker, Kent Atwood, and Jamal Warner all gave statements to the district attorney, stating that they had kept scores low in order to lose games. Their coach expressed shock and disappointment in his three top players, all of whom had hoped to . . ."

"What are you doing?" a voice spoke up right next to Nancy, making her jump about a foot in the air.

"Ned!" She breathed a sigh of relief as her boyfriend sat down, setting two glasses of soda on the table. "Thank goodness it's you. I was just . . ."

Her voice trailed off as the band stopped playing in midsong. Mel Lorenzo stepped up to the microphone, wearing a parka, hat, and scarf.

"Excuse me for the interruption," he said gruffly. "I'd like to see the members of the Omega Chi Epsilon team at the drinks counter right away."

"He sounds serious," Ned murmured.

"Maybe he found out something about the sabotage," Nancy said. Shoving the faxed papers back under the cover of Randy's notebook, she got to her feet. She and Ned made it to the counter at the same time as Grant, George, and C.J.

"What's going on?" C.J. asked.

Mr. Lorenzo unzipped his jacket with a yank. "I have reason to believe that someone from your team has broken Clues Challenge rules," he said.

"What!" Nancy, Ned, C.J., George, and Grant all cried at once.

"You know the rules. Searching for clues after sundown is forbidden," Mr. Lorenzo went on. "Yet on my way here I saw one of you in the woods near the library."

Nancy blinked at him. "That's impossible. We were all right here," she said.

"I know what I saw. Those yellow Omega hats are impossible to miss," Mr. Lorenzo insisted. He turned his eyes on each of them in turn. "I'm sorry, but as of this minute your team is disqualified from the Clues Challenge."

11

An Unfair Judgment

Nancy's mouth dropped open. "I don't know who you saw," she said, "but it wasn't any of us."

"We've all been here for at least half an hour," George added.

Mr. Lorenzo pulled off his parka and hat, and shook out his ponytail. "I'll need more than just your assurance," he told them. "You'll have to prove it."

Mr. Lorenzo scowled as Randy joined the group with his camera and notebook. Randy must have heard them talking because he said, "I saw them, Mr. Lorenzo. All five members of the Omega team have been here for some time now."

Sparks of irritation shot from Mr. Lorenzo's eyes. "You expect me to believe that?" he scoffed. "You reporters will say anything."

"He's not the only one who saw us," Grant said.

He, C.J., and Ned began pulling over other students. Mr. Lorenzo spoke to them one by one. After talking to about ten people, he waved the rest away.

"See, Mr. Lorenzo?" said Ned. "With all those people to back us up, you *have* to believe us."

Mr. Lorenzo nodded grudgingly. "All right. Omega Chi Epsilon is back in the Clues Challenge," he said.

"Does he have to sound so disappointed?" George whispered in Nancy's ear. "It's almost like he wants to disqualify us."

"Hmmm." Nancy turned to George and Ned and said, "I want to check something."

She led the way to the alcove where they had left their jackets. "We all wore our team hats tonight," she said. "If Mr. Lorenzo saw someone wearing one of the hats . . ."

"Then someone else must have taken one of them!" Ned finished. "Here!" he said, plucking two bright yellow Omega hats from the jumble of things. "C.J.'s and Grant's are still right here."

George scanned the rows of jackets and coats that were piled on top of one another. "Here's yours, Ned," she said, pulling out a green sleeve. "The hat's in your pocket."

Nancy finally found her own jacket. She reached in the pocket searching for her hat, but came up empty-handed.

"It's gone," she said.

George leaned against the wall. "So someone wore your hat to set us up to be disqualified," she said. "But . . . how could anyone know Mr. Lorenzo would see her?"

"Or him," Nancy said. "We don't know how yet. But maybe we can figure out *who*."

She stepped out of the alcove and looked over the party. "Dennis was here," she said as she caught sight of him near the band. "I saw him dancing a few minutes before Mr. Lorenzo got here."

"So he probably wasn't the person, because he couldn't be in two places at once," Ned said. "What about Joy?"

"She was here when we arrived. But not now. Do you guys see her anywhere?"

Ned and George shook their heads.

"We'd better make sure." Nancy pressed her mouth into a determined line and moved toward the other end of the room, where the band played. She, Ned, and George made their way up one side of the room and down the other.

"She's missing in action," Ned said. "Wait—scratch that." He nodded toward the entrance. "There she is."

Nancy turned in time to see Joy step out of the alcove where the coats were. "Her cheeks are bright red," Nancy murmured. "And look at the way she's

95

blowing on her hands—like she needs to warm them up after being outside."

Nancy, George, and Ned practically bowled over the people on the dance floor in their rush to get to Joy.

"I've been looking for you," Nancy said. "Where've you been?"

"Been?" Joy shot a cool glance at George and Ned, who had ducked into the alcove where the coats were. Ned reemerged a moment later, holding up a bright yellow Omega team hat.

"Look what I found in your jacket pocket, Nancy," he said, holding it up. "Your hat made a miraculous reappearance." He fixed Joy with a probing stare. "You wouldn't happen to know anything about that, would you?"

Joy's eyes flickered uncertainly. "I—I don't know what you're talking about," she said.

"Someone took Nancy's hat and did some clue searching in the woods near the library," George explained. "Our whole team was here, but nobody's seen *you* for a while. Now you reappear—and so does Nancy's hat."

Joy shook herself, and her uneasiness hardened to a look of cool arrogance. "I haven't broken any rules, and you know it," she said. "You act like victims. But if you ask me, *you're* the ones causing all the trouble around here." With that, she elbowed past Nancy and headed for the dance floor.

George stared blankly at Nancy and Ned. "Can someone explain what just happened?"

"Joy obviously isn't going to admit she took my hat," Nancy said. "I guess she knows we can't prove for sure it was her. But I still want to tell Mr. Lorenzo."

"Someone took my team hat," Nancy told Mr. Lorenzo. "Ten minutes ago we couldn't find my hat *or* Joy, but then the hat reappeared in my jacket pocket. Right after Joy turned up again."

Nancy wasn't surprised to see the doubt on Mr. Lorenzo's face. "I know it's not proof," she said quickly. "But you have to admit it's suspicious."

"I still don't have enough to disqualify anyone," he said, picking up his soda from the counter. "But I'll keep my eyes open."

"Thanks," Nancy said. She hesitated a moment, not sure how to phrase her next question. After all, she couldn't admit that she had sneaked into his office at the store. "About the threat I saw on your computer, are you *sure* it wasn't serious? No one is trying to blackmail you?"

Mr. Lorenzo's eyebrows shot up. "Your imagination is working overtime, Nancy," he said. "There's no threat. No blackmail."

This time Nancy knew he was lying. All she had to do now was find out why.

"What a day." Nancy yawned as she, Ned, and George walked back across the campus toward

97

Ned's frat. "We've been soaped, icicled, filed, disqualified, and reinstated—and we're *still* not done for the day."

George pushed up the cuff of her parka to check her watch. "What time did we tell C.J. and Grant we'd meet to brainstorm the third clue?" she asked.

"Nine-thirty," Ned said. He glanced at the brick fraternity house to their left, then chuckled. "I guess we're not the only ones working on clues."

"Sigma Pi," Nancy said, reading the Greek letters on the banner over the doorway. She glanced through the front window and saw Philip, Jake, and Malik. They were sitting around a wooden plank balanced on milk crates that served as their coffee table. On the plank was a slip of paper that looked like a clue.

"Where's Dennis?" she wondered out loud.

As she spoke, a door to the left of the living room opened. Dennis and the other guy on the Sigma Pi team emerged from a bedroom and joined everyone else.

"Did you guys see that bedroom? Do you think it's Dennis's?" Nancy asked.

Without waiting for an answer, she stepped off the path and waded through the snow toward the brick frat house.

"What are you doing?" George whispered.

Nancy made her way around the side of the house

to the window of the bedroom from which Dennis had emerged. "If he's the saboteur, maybe we'll find something to prove it in his room."

"We don't know for sure it *is* his room," Ned pointed out. He followed Nancy, shooting uncertain glances at the living room window. "What if they catch us?"

Nancy pushed the window frame up, then grinned when it rose noiselessly. "We'll have to make sure they don't, that's all."

"I'll keep watch," George whispered, ducking next to some bushes near the living room window. "Just be fast!"

Moving as quickly and quietly as they could, Nancy and Ned climbed through the window. To their left was a desk with a sleek laptop computer that Nancy recognized immediately.

"That's Dennis's. We're in luck!" she whispered.

The muffled sounds of Sigma Pi voices came through the door. Nancy took a calming breath and looked around at the bed, dresser, and bookshelf that took up most of the space. The walls were plastered with Emerson Wildcat pennants. Trophies, photographs, books, and papers cluttered every surface. A jumble of clothes and sports equipment was visible through the half-open closet door.

"I'll check in there," Ned whispered, tiptoing to the closet.

Nancy nodded. "Keep your eyes open for soap, a screwdriver, or any sign that Dennis is the one blackmailing Mr. Lorenzo."

She turned to the desk. Nancy didn't dare turn on the computer—Dennis would definitely hear it boot up. Instead she sorted through the books and papers on the desktop.

Nancy glanced at a couple of photographs as she set them aside to get at a notebook. One photo was of Dennis, a middle-aged couple, and a slightly older boy with dark eyebrows that stretched above his eyes in a solid line. Nancy guessed they were Dennis's brother and parents. The other was an autographed photo of Ziggy Laroquette, the hottest player in professional basketball. At the bottom of the photo someone had written a message: "The stars are in your reach. The sky's the limit." The signature, in the same slanted scrawl, read simply, "Pops."

Pops? Nancy knew Laroquette's nickname was the Rocket. Did that mean someone else had written that message?

Nancy forced herself to focus on the sabotage and blackmail. Putting the photo aside, she continued her search.

Notebooks, address book, schedule of football games . . .

She was just moving to the drawers when she heard Dennis's voice, right outside the door.

"I'll get my computer," he said. "I think I have a program that will . . ."

Nancy gasped. Ned straightened up from the closet like a bolt. His brown eyes locked on the door, widening as the doorknob rattled.

Dennis was about to catch them red-handed.

12

Close Call

Nancy watched helplessly as the doorknob twisted.

The sound of a door banging open made her jump. Her body went totally rigid—until she realized the door she'd heard wasn't the one to Dennis's room.

"Hello?" George's voice called out. "Dennis! I need to talk to you."

Nancy went limp. It must have been the front door of the frat that had been opened.

Go talk to George, Nancy begged silently. She kept her eyes on the bedroom door, hardly daring to breath. Please, don't come in now!

The knob stopped moving. "What do you want?" came Dennis's voice. Nancy heard his footsteps move away from the bedroom.

"Phew!" Nancy's whole body went limp with relief. "Let's get out of here!" she mouthed to Ned.

"Sorry to bother you, Dennis," George said, out in the living room. "It's just that, well, all these fraternities start to look the same after a while. Can you guys tell me which one is Omega?"

Nancy didn't stick around to listen to the rest. She and Ned climbed outside, shut the window behind them, and waited in the shadows of the frat house until George rejoined them.

The Omega Chi Epsilon frat house was just a few doors down Fraternity Row. When Nancy, George, and Ned got there, they saw C.J. just ahead of them.

"Your ankle's better?" Ned asked.

C.J. nodded, twirling his cane in the air. "My ankle doesn't hurt at all, and I don't need this anymore."

When they got inside, Grant was waiting for them in the common room—a large room with a fireplace and wood paneling.

"Ready?" he said, holding up a slip of paper. "The clue's right here."

Nancy and Ned flopped down on the couch next to Grant, while C.J. and George settled into a couple of battered chairs. Nancy shut her eyes and listened as Grant read the clue aloud.

" 'I am old and fat and wrinkled, yet people sing of my beauty,' " he began.

" 'I live on solid ground, but my head is in the clouds. . . .' "

As he spoke, Nancy tried to form a picture in her mind.

" 'I cannot speak,' " Grant continued, " 'yet I tell the stories of many, many people.

" 'I have rings, but you will find no fingers on me.' "

Nancy opened her eyes as Grant put the clue down on the coffee table in front of the couch. "That's it," he said. "Any ideas?"

Leaning forward, Nancy picked up the clue to study it. "Who can tell stories without speaking?" she wondered aloud.

"Maybe it's a *what*. Maybe a book?" Ned suggested.

"A notebook could have rings but no fingers," George said. "And I guess a book could be old and fat and wrinkled. . . ."

Grant frowned. "What about having its head in the clouds? That sounds more like a building."

His backpack was on the floor next to him. Grant pulled out his map of the Emerson campus. But as Nancy looked at it, she felt as if cotton was clogging her brain.

For forty-five minutes they tried to reason out the clue, but couldn't get it.

"Maybe we'll be able to think more clearly after we get some sleep," Nancy said, but she hated to end the day feeling so unsettled.

✿ ✿ ✿

Brrringgg!

Nancy's eyes popped open. She fumbled in the darkness to turn off the alarm, then groaned when she saw the glowing numbers on the clock: 4:30.

"Time to get up, already?" she mumbled, and lay quietly in the darkness.

"Rise and shine, sleepyhead," Nancy finally said, turning on the light on her bedside table.

George cracked one eye, then groaned and turned over, pulling the blankets over her head.

"Come on," Nancy said, laughing. "We only have an hour to get dressed, meet the guys for breakfast, and get to Clues Challenge headquarters before the horn blows at five-thirty."

She got out of bed and pulled on jeans and a turtleneck. "Now, where's my toothbrush and soap?"

Nancy grabbed her bag of toiletries from the windowsill, then paused with her hand in midair.

"Whoa," she murmured, staring at the gnarled branches of a maple tree that rose out of the snow outside the window. "A tree! That's the answer!"

"Come again?" George rubbed her eyes and swung her feet to the floor.

"A tree can be beautiful even when it's old and fat and wrinkled," Nancy said. "It can live on solid ground and still have its head in the clouds. It has rings . . ."

"But no fingers!" George jumped out of bed, suddenly wide-awake. "You're right! But what was the other part? Something about not speaking but telling stories . . ."

"That's the only part I'm not sure of," Nancy admitted. "Maybe the guys will know. They're a lot more familiar with the campus than we are."

It took them less than fifteen minutes to get dressed and drive to Ned's fraternity. They found Ned, C.J., and Grant in the kitchen making toast, scrambled eggs, and coffee.

"Hi, there," Ned said as the girls walked in. He stopped buttering toast long enough to give Nancy a big hug.

"Hi, yourself." Nancy leaned back and smiled up at his handsome face and dark eyes. "Do you guys know of any special trees on campus? Say, one that's big and old and wrinkled, and can tell many people's stories?"

"Of course!" Grant said, slapping his palm against his forehead. "The legendary oak!"

"What's that?" George asked.

"It's this huge oak way back in the woods on the other side of campus. It's been around since before Europeans settled here," Ned said. "It's a tradition to carve your initials on it."

"Which is how the tree tells the story of many people even though it can't speak," said George.

C.J. nodded, grinning from ear to ear. "When Mr. Lorenzo blows the horn this time," he said, "no one's going to stop us!"

* * *

A pale light was just snaking across the horizon when Mr. Lorenzo sounded his air horn at five-thirty sharp.

The Omegas were ready. Within five minutes they had put on their skis and left the Sports Complex behind.

"Did you see Joy's face when we shot out of there?" Grant said, grinning. "She couldn't believe we solved the clue before she did."

C.J. slid forward on his skis, heading toward the woods on the far side of the lake. He angled a quick glance back at Randy, who was skiing behind him. "It's more than five miles to the oak," he said. "You're sure you're up for the trip?"

Randy nodded. "Absolutely. As long as we can talk while we ski," he said. "I was hoping you could tell me about the Clues Challenge sponsor."

"Mr. Lorenzo?" C.J. skied forward easily. Nancy was glad to see his ankle didn't seem to trouble him. "There's not much to tell. He just opened SportsMania a few months ago."

"What about before that?" Randy asked.

"Beats me," C.J. said.

As she skied behind Randy, Nancy wondered at his questions. "I thought your article was about C.J., not Mr. Lorenzo," she said.

"Background information is an important part of any article. I like to get my facts straight," he told her.

But as they skied deeper into the woods, Randy's

questions continued to focus on Mr. Lorenzo. Did he have a special interest in college sports? Did C.J. know how long Mr. Lorenzo had lived in Emerson, or where he moved from?

After a while Nancy tuned him out and concentrated on skiing. The path they forged was through dense forest. Every time Nancy breathed in, she smelled the sweet fragrance of cedar and pine.

"I think we're getting close," Ned said.

Nancy began a searching sweep over the area with her eyes. There were plenty of oaks, but none that looked as big as the one Ned had described.

"You think we took a wrong turn somewhere?" George wondered, when they'd been skiing for more than forty-five minutes. "I don't see—"

"There!" Nancy stopped in her tracks and pointed with her ski pole.

About twenty yards in front of her the branches of a huge oak towered over the other treetops. As they skied toward it, Nancy saw a massive tree trunk more than four feet across. Its bark was chipped and scarred from carvings that covered nearly every square inch of it.

"That's the legendary oak, all right," Grant confirmed.

Nancy saw a second set of ski tracks leading up to the legendary oak. They snaked through the woods from somewhere to the left of the path the Omegas had taken.

"Whoever made those took a different route through the woods," George commented.

"Jimmy, probably," Grant said. "He hid the clues for Mr. Lorenzo."

C.J. tilted his face upward and then said, "There's the snowflake."

Nancy looked up, following his gaze. In the top-most branches of the tree, sunlight glinted off a plastic snowflake.

"This one's mine," she said. After stepping out of her skis, she hoisted herself on to the lowest branch. She reached for the next branch, then had to grab it wildly as her boot slipped on the icy bark.

"Whoa!" she cried.

"Careful, Nan," George called.

Nancy steadied herself, flashing a grin down at her teammates. "Don't worry," she assured them.

Slowly and surely, she climbed up to the next branch, and the next. She noticed that snow had already been cleared from some of the branches—no doubt by Jimmy when he had hidden the clue. Footing on those branches was less slippery than where the snow was still thick, so Nancy followed the trail upward. She didn't pause until she saw the treetops of the evergreens that were thick around the oak.

"Wow!" she murmured.

Straight down, Ned and the others looked tiny. Nancy felt so giddy she had to clutch the branch even tighter to keep her balance.

"Almost there." She angled a look up at the plastic snowflake, which glowed in the sunlight just two branches over her head.

Taking a deep breath, she placed her boot on the next branch and pulled herself up. She steadied herself, then reached for a higher branch.

With a chilling, cracking sound, the branch beneath her gave way. Nancy gasped as her boot slipped off.

"Noooo!" she cried.

In the next instant she felt herself falling into thin air.

13

Into Thin Air

Nancy plummeted downward. Her heart stopped in her chest as she caught a dizzying glimpse of snow-covered trees far below.

Throwing her arms out, she grabbed a branch and her body jerked to a stop.

"Ooooh!" Nancy's arms felt as if they had been yanked from their sockets.

"Nancy!" Shouts of alarm rose up from below.

Grunting, Nancy swung her legs around to grab the tree trunk with them. Her hands started to slip on the icy branch, and she wasn't sure how she did it, but at last she was sitting firmly on a solid branch.

"I'm . . . all right!" she called down, her chest heaving.

"What happened?" Ned's worried voice rose up to her.

Nancy looked up, eyeing the broken branch. It had split just inches from the trunk. Now the branch hung at right angles to its original position, exposing the pale, splintered wood beneath the heavy bark.

After taking a few deep breaths, Nancy climbed up for a closer look. She frowned when she saw the smooth slice in the wood. The cut ran about two thirds of the way through.

Someone had sawn through the branch.

Nancy shivered, thinking of what might have happened if she hadn't stopped her fall. Then, pushing the thought firmly from her head, she climbed the rest of the way to the plastic snowflake and opened it.

Four paper clues lay folded inside. So we're the first team to get the clue, thought Nancy. But someone came here first and cut through that branch.

Nancy climbed quickly back to the ground.

"I was so scared for you," Ned said, giving her a hug. "That could have been a nasty accident."

"It wasn't an accident," Nancy told him. "Someone sawed through that branch."

"What!" Ned, C.J., Grant, George, and Randy all cried at the same time.

"Oh, man." C.J. shook his head in disgust. "Someone has tried to stop us from getting every single clue."

"But who?" George wondered aloud. "Joy?"

Nancy had been running over the list of suspects

in her own mind. "I'm pretty sure Joy is the one who took my hat," she said. "Maybe this is what she did in the woods last night."

"What about Dennis?" Grant asked. "He went AWOL when his teammates were brainstorming the second clue yesterday. He could have come here then and sawed through the branch."

"But how could Dennis have known where this snowflake was hidden?" Ned asked. "As of this morning, his team didn't even have the clue from the administration building."

Nancy grabbed her ski pole and poked the snow with it while she thought. "Someone tried to threaten Mr. Lorenzo into handing over the answers to the clues. Maybe it was Dennis," she suggested.

"Maybe," said George. "But if Dennis got all the answers, why is his team so far behind in the Clues Challenge?"

It was a question for which Nancy didn't have an answer.

Nancy shot a surreptitious glance at Randy as she pulled her yellow team hat farther down on her head. Was *he* the blackmailer and saboteur?

She shook herself. It was a pretty far-fetched theory. So far, the only thing implicating Randy was Mr. Lorenzo's intense dislike of him.

"Heads up, everyone. Look who's here," said C.J., breaking into her thoughts.

Nancy looked up to see Joy ski toward them

through the woods. Hanna and the three other girls from Delta Tau stretched in a line behind her, skiing forward at a spirited pace.

"Looks like we're ahead this time," C.J. said to Joy as she came to a stop next to him. He nodded toward the slip of paper in Nancy's hand.

"Not for long." Joy gave a shrug, glancing at the clue. She popped off her skis and dropped her backpack. "I'll be back in a flash."

"Be careful near the top," Nancy warned. "There's a broken branch."

"Someone sawed through most of it, so it would snap when it was stepped on," George added.

Joy's face was hidden from view as she pulled herself up onto the lowest branch. When she finally glanced down at Nancy, Joy's eyes flashed with irritation. "I suppose you're going to try to pin that on me, too?" she said.

She reached calmly for the next branch and kept climbing. Her teammates gathered at the foot of the tree calling encouragement.

"She sure doesn't act like she's guilty," George whispered in Nancy's ear.

"No, but maybe that's exactly what she's doing . . . *acting*," said Nancy.

She eyed Joy's teammates. All their faces were turned upward. No one was paying attention to Joy's backpack, which lay on a mound of snow next to her skis.

Catching George's eye, Nancy held her finger to her lips. She moved quietly to the backpack. Crouching next to it, she pulled the zipper open slowly.

Hmm, she thought, scanning the contents. Joy had packed an extra pair of gloves, sunglasses, protective lip balm. . . . Nancy saw nothing unusual—until her gaze landed on a small bottle with a prescription label.

She glanced quickly over her shoulder. Seeing that Joy was hidden by the branches of the huge old oak, Nancy reached inside the pack and pulled out the bottle.

The prescription label was partly torn. Nancy couldn't read the name of the person it was for. But the name of the medicine was still intact.

"Comptamine," Nancy breathed. The same drug that was used to spike their dessert at the pre-Challenge dinner!

Gripping the bottle tightly, she made her way to her teammates, who waited next to their skis.

"Find something?" Grant guessed, looking at the bottle.

Nancy showed them the prescription bottle, then turned as Joy's teammates cheered. "Joy's on her way down with the clue," she said, peering up into the towering branches of the oak.

"Good." Ned frowned, stomping the snow under his boots. " 'Cause she's got some explaining to do."

"What's going on?" asked Hanna, a girl with freckles and a halo of reddish brown curls around her face. She glanced curiously at the Omega team as they circled Joy at the foot of the legendary oak.

"I found this in your backpack, Joy," Nancy began. She opened the container and poured a handful of chalky tablets into her palm.

Joy stared blankly at the tablets, her pale brows knit together. "Pills?" she said. "But I don't—"

"It's the same medicine someone used to spike our dessert at the Eatery," C.J. cut in. "Don't try to pretend you don't recognize them. They're obviously yours, Joy."

Joy's eyes flickered uncertainly. "I've never . . ." Her voice trailed off as Randy snapped a photograph of her.

"Hey!" she said sharply. "I don't like being set up—especially in front of the press!"

She grabbed the bottle of pills and shook them in front of Nancy's face. "You know these aren't mine. Why are you setting me up?"

Whoa, thought Nancy. Joy was hardly acting like a person who'd been caught red-handed.

"You're going to be in serious trouble when we show this to Mr. Lorenzo," George pointed out.

"And the police," Nancy added.

"But I didn't do anything!" Joy insisted.

"Are you saying you're *not* the person Mr. Lorenzo saw sneaking around the woods in my hat?" she asked, turning back to Joy. "That you *weren't* up on the roof on the administration building when that icicle was knocked off?"

"And what about the other night, when we saw you at the bell tower," George added. "You were definitely up to something there."

Joy bit her lip. She glanced back at her teammates. All four girls watched her uncertainly.

"All right. All right," Joy said at last, letting out her breath in a sigh of frustration. "I *have* been up to something. But it's not what you think. It doesn't have anything to do with the Clues Challenge!"

Nancy couldn't believe how defiant Joy was. "We're listening," Nancy said.

"There's a chemistry midterm coming up," Joy began. "I promised to help someone in my class study. That's who I was meeting after the pre-Challenge dinner. I was going to lend her my study notes."

"Outside the bell tower, in the freezing cold?" George asked doubtfully. "Why did your *friend* run away like she was harboring top-secret classified information? Getting class notes is no big deal."

"It is to my friend," Joy insisted. "She's used to being at the top of her class. I guess she figured her reputation as a brainiac would be wrecked if people knew she'd been having trouble."

Nancy searched her mind, trying to fit Joy's explanation to all that had happened. There were still too many unanswered questions. "What about your glove?" Nancy asked.

"The one I found on the roof of the administration building," Ned reminded Joy. "Along with that file.

117

Are you trying to say you didn't use the file to sabotage George's skis?"

Joy shook her head forcefully. "I didn't! I was never on that roof, I never touched that screwdriver, and I don't know about any pills," she insisted. Planting her hands on her hips, she fixed Nancy with accusing eyes. "Someone set me up!"

She seemed so sincerely angry that Nancy found herself believing Joy. "What about my yellow Omega team hat? I know you took it," Nancy said.

For the first time Joy's defiant glare faded to uncertainty. "That *was* me," she admitted. "Since you guys wrecked my first chance to give my friend the chemistry notes, I had to make another rendezvous. I decided to meet her during the party, when everyone from the Clues Challenge would be at the Attic."

"That way no one would see you outside and think you were searching for clues," Grant said.

"Exactly," Joy said, nodding. "I didn't plan to take your hat, Nancy. But as I was on my way out of the Attic, I saw it sticking out of your jacket pocket. . . ." She took a deep breath and let it out in a cloudy stream. "I was really mad at you guys."

"Why?" C.J. asked.

"You kept accusing me of things I didn't do! I was sure you were trying to make *me* look bad, so I decided to give you a taste of your own medicine. I took the yellow Omega hat for extra insurance. That way if anyone happened to see me by the boathouse . . ."

"We would get the blame instead of you," Nancy finished.

Joy nodded. "Look, I'm sorry you almost got disqualified," she said. "But I'm not the one who's been sabotaging you guys. And I'm not about to waste time on this stuff now." Turning to her teammates, she held up the clue she'd brought down from the top of the oak tree. "Let's go, Deltas!"

Joy and her teammates waded through the snow to their skis, put them on, and skied back the way they had come.

"What are we waiting for?" C.J. asked, jumping for his own skis. "Let's finish going over the evidence *after* we win the Clues Challenge!"

The Omega team stayed close on the Deltas' trail as they skied back toward Clues Challenge headquarters. Nancy let the thrill of the race take over her thoughts about the sabotage. She didn't think about the case again until they reached the Sports Complex.

Everyone headed for the glassed-in atrium—except Randy. He held back, hoisting his skis and poles onto his shoulder. "I'll catch up with you later, C.J.," he said. "I've got some business to take care of."

There was a determined note in his voice that caught Nancy's attention. Randy looked long and hard at the atrium, where Mr. Lorenzo sat.

"Did you see the way he looked at Mr. Lorenzo?" Nancy whispered to George and Ned as Randy started toward his Jeep. "You guys brainstorm the

119

clue without me," she said. "I want to find out what Randy is up to."

Ned nodded, taking her skis and poles. "We'll be at the Student Center," he told her.

George stuck her skis into the snow next to Ned and hustled to catch up with Nancy. "Well, you didn't think I'd let you go by yourself, did you?"

The two girls ran inside the atrium to pull off their ski boots and grab their own shoes. By the time they got into Nancy's Mustang, Randy was just turning his Jeep onto the main road of the campus. Nancy followed at a distance.

"He's leaving campus," George said.

Up ahead, Randy's Jeep turned right onto Main Street. He drove past the Eatery, then turned left just past SportsMania and parked on a side street. Nancy pulled over to the curb a few cars back, and she and George watched through the windshield.

Randy got out of his Jeep and jogged across the street. He looked both ways, then ducked into an alleyway.

"Talk about suspicious," George murmured.

Nancy reached for the door handle and pulled it. "Let's follow him," she said.

She and George crossed over to the alleyway and paused at the end of it. Nancy peeked her head around for a look, then blinked to let her eyes adjust to the dimmer light.

The alley stretched back about fifty feet, she saw.

One side of it ran behind the businesses on Main Street. Windows dotted the grungy brick walls, along with a network of fire escapes higher up.

Randy was about halfway down the alleyway. As Nancy watched, he reached up toward one of the windows and pushed it up.

"He's sneaking in!" she whispered to George.

"Where?" she asked.

"SportsMania, I bet." Nancy frowned as Randy hoisted himself up and over the windowsill. As soon as he was out of sight, she darted into the alleyway. "Come on!" she whispered.

They tiptoed down the alleyway, then crouched beneath the window Nancy had seen him climb through. They heard drawers opening, and the rustle of papers.

"Come on," Randy's muttered voice came through the window.

Slowly and silently Nancy lifted her head until she could see through the window. They were at the back of SportsMania, all right. Nancy recognized Mel Lorenzo's cluttered office immediately. Her eyes narrowed as she caught sight of Randy, bent over an open drawer of Mr. Lorenzo's desk.

"Ahem!" Nancy cleared her throat.

Randy's head jerked upward, and his surprised eyes locked on her.

Nancy was through the window in a flash. "Gotcha," she said.

121

14

Caught!

"What are you doing?" George demanded of Randy, scrambling through the window behind Nancy. "Leaving Mr. Lorenzo another blackmail note?"

"Shhh!" Randy held a finger to his lips, jerking his head toward the office door. "If Jimmy hears, we'll *all* be in hot water."

The three of them froze. Nancy didn't relax until she heard Jimmy talking to a customer in the store. He didn't appear to have heard them.

"Don't try to change the subject," she whispered, crossing her arms over her chest. "We were talking about blackmail, remember?"

Randy stared at her blankly. "I don't know what you mean," he said.

"Shouldn't we call the police, Nancy?" George bit her lip and leaned against a stack of cardboard cartons.

"Wait!" Randy glanced quickly back and forth between Nancy and George. "Just hear me out. If you still want to call the police when I'm done, I won't stop you."

Nancy glanced at George, who shrugged. "Okay," Nancy said.

"I'm looking for evidence," Randy said. "Evidence that could lead to the capture of a criminal who's been on the loose for the past three years."

He pulled his notebook from his parka pocket. Nancy recognized the faxed sheets he slipped out from under the cover and held out to her.

"Three years ago there was a point-fixing scam at Western Tech," Randy explained. "I wrote about it for *Sports World.*"

Nancy said nothing to let on that she had already read the beginning of the article. Holding it out so George could see it, too, she skipped over the part she had already seen.

"Whoa," she said, reading farther. "The man who masterminded the scam got away?"

Randy nodded. "Andrew Papazian, a local businessman. He skipped bail and was never seen or heard from again."

"So those three college kids were ruined," George said, pointing at the names in the article. "Ty

123

Brubaker, Kent Atwood, and Jamal Warner. But Papazian got away."

"Actually . . ." Randy shot another glance at the closed office door. Lowering his voice even more, he said, "I think I may have found him."

Nancy's mouth fell open as she made the connection. "Mr. Lorenzo? You think *he's* Andrew Papazian?"

"There's a photograph in the article." George flipped to the second page and pointed at the grainy image.

"Hmm." Nancy looked closely, then frowned. "See how fat Papazian is?" She pointed to the huge paunch on the man in the photograph. He held a corner of his suit jacket over his face. A fat cigar stuck out from between the fingers of his right hand, which he used to hold a corner of his suit jacket over his face. "Mr. Lorenzo is in much better shape than that. And I've never seen him smoke."

"I know, I know. Papazian didn't wear a ponytail or tinted glasses, either," Randy said. "But he could have changed the way he looked so no one would recognize him. Try to see past the superficial details."

Nancy stared at the photo again. "Papazian is big, like Mr. Lorenzo," she said slowly. "If this guy lost weight, got in shape, gave up cigars, grew his hair, and started wearing glasses, he *could* look like Mr. Lorenzo."

"That's a lot of *if*s," George said. She fixed Randy

with questioning eyes as she put the faxed article down on the desk.

"I didn't make the connection at first, either," Randy told them. "But there was something Lorenzo kept saying, 'Man, oh, man.' " Randy tapped the article against the desk. "It rang a bell. Then I remembered where I'd heard it."

"Andrew Papazian?" Nancy guessed.

"Bingo," said Randy. "He used that expression all the time. During the trial, press conferences . . . I wasn't the only person who noticed. After he skipped town, I remember reading a newspaper headline that said, 'Papazian Is Gone, Oh, Gone!' "

"I still couldn't say for sure that Mr. Lorenzo is the same person in that photograph," Nancy said. "But if he *is*, that could explain why he's being blackmailed. Someone else could have realized he was Andrew Papazian."

"And that person threatened to spill the beans— unless Mr. Lorenzo paid big money," George finished. "The big question is, who is the person?"

Nancy rested her hands on the desk and leaned over them, thinking. "I don't know. And I'm still not sure what all this has to do with the sabotage that's been going on at the Clues Challenge," she said. "Maybe nothing."

Randy's article lay on the desk in front of her. Nancy found herself staring at a photograph near the end of the article, of the three Western Tech basketball players who had been expelled.

The caption read, "Ty Brubaker, Kent Atwood, and Jamal Warner expressed remorse for their part in the point-fixing scandal. Ty Brubaker, former high scorer for Western Tech, said, 'It was wrong. I'm sorry I ever let Pops talk me into it.' "

"Pops?" Nancy said, fingering the print.

"Papazian's nickname," Randy told her.

"I've see it before . . . somewhere," Nancy murmured.

She couldn't take her eyes off the photograph. There was something familiar about it. She kept going back to Ty Brubaker, and the dark brows that stretched over his eyes in a thick line. . . .

"That's it!" she said, snapping her fingers.

"Shhh!" George shot a warning glance at the door.

All three of them froze. Nancy only relaxed when she heard Jimmy and his customer still talking out in the store.

"There's a photograph of Dennis and Ty Brubaker in Dennis's room!" she whispered. "He has an autographed photograph of Ziggy Laroquette, too. Someone named Pops wrote on it."

"Papazian?" George guessed.

Nancy shrugged. "Maybe. But we know one thing for sure. If Dennis knew Ty Brubaker, he definitely knows about the point-fixing."

"Which means he could have known Papazian before he skipped bail and turned himself into Mr. Lorenzo." Randy jumped to his feet and headed for the window. "Dennis is the link we need to put Papazian behind bars where he belongs. I've got to talk to him."

"Hold it!" Nancy said. "We still don't know for sure that Mr. Lorenzo and Andrew Papazian are the same person."

"Besides which," George added, "Dennis might not want to cooperate. If he's the person who's been blackmailing Mr. Lorenzo, he's made a lot of money by keeping Papazian's identity a secret."

Randy shoved the faxed article under the cover of his notebook and dropped it into his jacket pocket. "We can't sit by and do nothing. If Lorenzo is Papazian, he belongs in jail."

"We need to find out the truth," Nancy said. "Let's talk to Dennis."

"How? We don't know where he is," George said.

Nancy headed for the window and began to climb back out to the alley. "I think I know how we can find out."

Ten minutes later Nancy turned her Mustang into the parking lot of the Sports Complex. She waved to Randy and George, who continued down Campus Road toward the Student Center in Randy's Jeep.

"Here goes." Nancy parked, got out of her car, and started toward the glassed-in atrium.

If anyone knew where Dennis was, it was Mel Lorenzo. He had been keeping track of each team's progress during the Clues Challenge. Nancy knew she had to be careful not to arouse his suspicion, though. That was why she, George, and Randy had decided it would be best if she went alone to talk to Mr. Lorenzo while they went to the Student Center to bring the rest of the team up to speed.

Nancy pulled open the door to the atrium and went inside. Mr. Lorenzo looked up at her from his table, then glanced curiously behind her. "Did you lose the rest of your team?" he asked.

"I thought they might be here, solving the last clue," Nancy fibbed. She pretended to be surprised not to see her teammates. "They didn't already head out to get the banner, did they?"

"Man, oh, man. No one's gotten that far," Mr. Lorenzo said, letting out a laugh.

"I guess we'd better hurry then, if we want to keep ahead of the other teams," Nancy said. She quickly scanned the equipment—then blinked when she saw the melted snow that dripped from the Sigmas' cross-country skis. "The Sigmas already got the clue from the old oak tree?" she asked.

Mr. Lorenzo nodded. "Skied back about ten minutes ago," he told her.

That was fast, thought Nancy, checking her watch. It had only been two and a half hours since Mr.

Lorenzo had blown the whistle to start that day's competition. Yet the Sigmas had managed to get the clue from outside the administration building, solve it, and ski all the way to the old oak and back. It seemed next to impossible.

Unless Dennis already had the answers to the clues, Nancy thought.

"Everything all right?" Mr. Lorenzo's voice cut into her thoughts.

Nancy shook herself and forced a smile. "Fine," she told him.

At least now she had a better idea of where Dennis might be. He and his teammates were probably solving the last clue.

So our best chance of finding Dennis, she thought, is to solve the clue ourselves and catch up to him where the banner is hidden.

"See you later, Mr. Lorenzo!" Nancy called.

She sprinted for the door. But as she burst out into the cold air, she felt his watchful eyes upon her.

No sooner did Nancy enter the Student Center than she heard someone call her name.

"Nancy! Over here."

Ned waved to her from a bank of computers that ran along the wall just inside the massive wooden doors. He, George, C.J., and Randy crowded around a terminal while Grant sat at the keyboard. "We've got the answer to the last clue!"

"Great!" Jogging over, Nancy read the clue that lay right next to the keyboard:

REJ - 29
BP - 30
LS - 42
HL - 63
SM - 66

High atop their Hall of Fame
The victory banner lies.
Beyond the vents, beneath the snow,
Our happy-sad medal marks the spot.
Go quickly, challengers, find your way in.
Good luck to all, and may the best team win.

"We figured out those letters are initials," C.J. said. "At first we thought they were top players in some sport, and that those numbers were from their jerseys."

"That would fit with the reference to the Hall of Fame," Nancy said.

George pointed farther down the list of clues. "But look here, at the part about the happy-sad medal," she said. "That made us think about the Drama Club."

"Right!" said Nancy. "The happy and sad masks are the symbol for theater."

"We found out that the Drama Club has their own Hall of Fame," Grant explained. "I checked their Web site. In 1929 Rose Ellis Johnston was voted in.

In 1930 it was Brian Peters. Linda Schmidt in 1942 . . . You get the idea."

Nancy ran her finger down the list of initials at the top of the clue. "REJ, BP, LS . . . You guys are brilliant!" she crowed. "According to this, the banner is somewhere high up, where there are vents and snow."

"The Drama Club Hall of Fame is in the MacClaren Performance Center," Ned said. "We were just waiting for you to get here so we can head over there and look on the roof."

Nancy grabbed the clue and shoved it in her pocket. "Excellent! I found out that Dennis's team is working on solving the last clue, too. Let's hope we can catch up to him at the performance center."

"Randy told us about how he thinks Mr. Lorenzo is that guy Papazian—and about how Dennis might be blackmailing him." C.J. frowned as he pulled on his parka and zipped it.

"We need to find out for sure," Nancy said.

As she pulled on her team hat, she caught sight of Dede, Krista, Rosie, and the rest of the Kappa team.

"We finally got the clue from the administration building," Dede said, holding up a slip of paper with a grin.

"Good luck," Nancy told her. She headed for the doors, then paused with her hand on the carved wood. "Have you guys seen Dennis?" she called back to the Kappas.

Krista rolled her eyes. "That guy is so full of himself. He practically bowled us over outside the administration building just now. He just kept going. No sorry. No excuse me. Nothing."

"Which way was he headed?" Grant asked.

"East," Dede said. "Toward the dorms."

Grant took the campus map from his backpack and looked at it. "The MacClaren Center is in the total opposite direction from where he was going," he said, frowning.

"We'd better split up," Nancy said. "Grant, you're the best climber. You'd better head over to the Mac-Claren Center to get the banner."

"I'll go with him," C.J. offered.

"The rest of us can look for Dennis on the east side of campus," Nancy said. She took the map Grant held out, then pushed through the wooden door into the bright sunshine. "Let's go!"

"What about the police? Shouldn't we tell them what we suspect?" George asked.

"Let's wait till we find Dennis," Ned said. "He's the one we need to talk to."

Nancy scanned the map of the campus as she, Ned, George, and Randy headed east. Grant was right about the MacClaren Center, she realized. It was on the far western side of campus, not far from Fraternity Row. Dennis must have been going somewhere else. . . .

"But where?" Nancy murmured. She ran her finger over the buildings on the east side of campus. One of the dorms? The Academic Quad?

"What's this?" she asked, pointing to a square on the map that wasn't labeled.

Ned glanced over Nancy's shoulder at the spot. "That's the old theater building. It's been abandoned for years, but I heard the college is planning to turn it into rehearsal space for the music department."

"There's an *old* theater building?" Nancy pulled the clue from her pocket and skimmed it. "Oh, my gosh . . . Look at the years next to the initials. The most recent one is 1966. How old is the MacClaren Center?"

Ned frowned. "It just opened last year."

"Which means the Clues Challenge banner isn't there. It's on the roof of the *old* theater building!" George picked up her pace, jogging forward on the snowy path. "We'd better hurry if we want to catch up with Dennis."

Ten minutes later they angled around the bell tower, and the building came into sight. It was five stories tall, with boarded-up windows and crumbling bricks.

"That fire escape is ancient," George said, jogging through the snow toward the building. "It looks like it's rusted totally through in some spots. I don't know if we should risk climbing it."

Nancy's eyes flew over the area, taking in every detail. "Footprints!" she said, following the prints off the path. "They go around to the other side of the building."

She, Ned, George, and Randy kicked through the snow, following the footprints. As they rounded the corner of the building, Nancy's eyes fell on a thick rope dangling from the roof.

"Someone's up there, all right," George said.

"It's got to be Dennis." Randy reached into his jacket pocket, then frowned. "I've got a cell phone in my Jeep," he said. "I'll call the police."

Nancy watched him jog back the way they had come. Then she took hold of the rope and started to climb. She placed a boot carefully against the wall and pulled herself up with the rope, angling her body out from the bricks.

"Steady," George called as Nancy's boot slipped on the snowy wall.

Step by snowy step, Nancy made her way upward. Wind whipped her hair over her eyes, and her fingers felt stiff and numb. But finally she grabbed the top bricks and pulled herself on to the roof. As soon as she let go of the rope, it went taut again. It would just be a few minutes before Ned and George made it up to join her, but Nancy decided not to wait for them.

She looked out over the roof. A series of vents and towers blocked her view. Nancy followed the footprints, circling around the obstacles until she was finally able to see the far side of the roof.

"Dennis!" she called.

He was bent over a wooden crate near the far wall.

"Huh?" Dennis jerked upright, shooting a surprised glance at Nancy. In his left hand was a wooden medallion, with two masks painted on it in gold, one happy and one sad.

Nancy's mind raced a mile a minute. She still didn't know for sure that Dennis was behind the blackmail *or* the sabotage. But she decided to take a chance.

"Tell me something, Dennis," she said. "When did you realize Mr. Lorenzo was really Andrew Papazian?" she asked.

Dennis's mouth fell open. "How did you know?"

Yes! thought Nancy. Dennis's slip confirmed it. Mr. Lorenzo *was* Andrew Papazian. And Dennis definitely knew his real identity.

"Blackmail is a serious crime, Dennis," she went on.

"One you're going to jail for," Ned added, appearing next to Nancy.

Dennis's mouth hardened into a tight, angry line. "Oh, yeah?" he challenged.

In three powerful strides he plowed through the snow to the edge of the roof. He sent a puff of white powder flying into the air as he slid his legs over the side. For a second he balanced on the edge, with the lower part of his body hanging out of sight.

135

"What are you doing?" Nancy called over to him. "You'll hurt yourself!"

"You think I'm going to jail?" Dennis countered. Sparks of challenge shot from his eyes. "You'll have to catch me first."

With that, he slipped the rest of the way over the edge of the roof and disappeared from sight.

15

Over the Edge

"No!" Nancy vaulted toward the spot where Dennis had gone over.

"What happened?" George's breathless voice came from behind her. "Where's Dennis?"

Nancy glanced over her shoulder just long enough to see George wade through the snowdrift toward Ned. Nancy slid to a stop inches from the edge, weaving back and forth to catch her balance. "He's using the old fire escape!" she called.

Just below Nancy, Dennis's black parka stood out against the snow-covered fire escape. He gripped the rusted metal railing, sending showers of snow into the air. The fire escape groaned and shook unsteadily with his every step. Nancy gasped when his boot actually broke through the brittle metal.

137

"Whoa!" Dennis caught himself. Clutching the railing, he pulled his boot up, then slipped, slid, and stumbled down the creaky iron stairs to the fourth-floor level.

"That thing's a death trap!" Ned said, coming up beside Nancy.

But she was already lowering herself over the edge of the roof. "I'm going after him," she said.

She dropped to the highest platform, doing her best to ignore the screech of metal as the fire escape pulled at the metal pins anchored in the crumbling bricks. "Dennis, stop!" she called.

His head jerked upward. "Not a chance," he said.

He moved faster along the rusted metal strips that formed the fire escape floor. His steps made the fire escape shake even more unsteadily.

Nancy let out a frustrated groan as Dennis made his way down the rickety stairs to the third level. "I've got to catch up!" she muttered, clattering down the unsteady metal steps to the fourth level. He was just one floor below her now. But between the snow and the crumbling weak spots . . .

How can I catch up with him? her mind screamed. It didn't seem possible.

"Unless . . ."

Nancy crouched down at the very edge of the fire escape. The iron there seemed fairly stable. If she was lucky, it would take the stress of what she was about to do.

She got her hands around the metal in as firm a grip as she could. Holding on tight, she shot her legs out into the air, letting her body fall so she swung below the fourth-floor level.

For one terrifying moment, her body swung outside the fire escape and there was nothing at all to break her fall.

Don't slip, she begged silently. Please don't slip.

"Nancy!" she heard George cry out. "What are you doing!"

Then Nancy swung back and saw the rusted iron of the fire escape below her again. Letting go, she dropped to the third-floor level of the fire escape. She landed right in front of Dennis with a thud that caused the whole fire escape to shudder and shriek.

"What—?" A look of total shock registered on Dennis's face. But it disappeared a split-second later as Nancy's left boot broke right through the fragile iron floor.

Even as she whirled off-balance, Nancy was determined not to let Dennis get away. She grabbed the front of his parka and managed to pull her boot out of the gaping hole. But as she did so, she pushed Dennis into the metal railing.

With an awful scraping sound the entire railing gave way behind him. Dennis began to fall backward, his face filled with panic. A huge wave of fear swept over Nancy as she felt herself being pulled along with him.

"Nooo!" she cried.

139

Bracing her feet, she angled her body away from the gaping hole in the railing. She pulled on Dennis's parka with all she had. For a fraction of a second, she wasn't sure she could do it. Then they both stumbled back against the wall of the building.

"Everyone all right?" Ned's worried voice called down.

It took Nancy a moment to realize that she and Dennis were both unharmed. Dennis was crouched next to her, his hands on his knees.

"Fine," she called, then turned back to Dennis.

His dark eyes flew from the gaping hole in the railing, to the rusted iron strips of the rest of the fire escape. Nancy got the feeling he was still gauging his chances of getting away.

"Don't even think about it," she said. "Randy's called the police. They'll be here any minute. It's over, Dennis."

He shot one last desperate glimpse downward, then sagged heavily against the brick wall. "Okay. Okay."

Nancy gulped as the fire escape shifted with a creaky groan. "Let's get off this thing," she said.

She gestured for Dennis to go ahead of her. As he started to move, Nancy thought back over all that had happened in the last two days. There were still some blanks, but if she played her cards right, maybe she could get Dennis to fill them in for her.

"You've been blackmailing Mr. Lorenzo since early October?" she asked, stepping carefully around the hole where her boot had broken through the metal. Seeing the surprised look he shot at her, she explained, "I saw the note you left him, telling him that your price was going up to fifteen hundred dollars. And his ledger showed unexplained payments made every fourteen days. It didn't take a genius to put the two together."

Dennis glowered. "I deserved that money, after what Pops did to my brother," he said.

"Ty Brubaker?" Nancy guessed, remembering the photograph she'd seen in his room.

"Yeah," he told her. "He's my half brother, actually. Ty worshiped Pops."

"You mean, Andrew Papazian?" Nancy said.

"That's right. Pops promised to be Ty's manager when he went pro," Dennis explained. "He got Ty an autographed picture of the Rocket and said he could make Ty an even bigger star." He frowned, testing an icy spot on the fire escape before stepping past it. "Ty didn't feel right about the point-fixing, but Pops talked him into it, said he'd make sure no one ever found out."

Nancy tried to ignore the groaning metal as she followed Dennis up the stairs. "He must have felt really betrayed when Papazian skipped town."

"Leaving Ty and the other players to take the rap," Dennis said, blowing out an angry breath. "I couldn't believe it when I walked into SportsMania and saw him. Lorenzo looked different, but I'd seen Pops enough not to be fooled by the glasses and extra muscle. I told him right away I was going to tell the cops."

His angry fist came down on the railing, making it shudder and groan.

Nancy forced herself to focus on the conversation. "What happened?" she asked. "He talked you out of it?"

"He offered to pay me to keep quiet." Dennis angled a defiant look down at her. "Do you blame me for saying yes? A thousand dollars, every two weeks. That's serious cash!"

"Enough to make up for what Papazian did to Ty?" Nancy asked quietly. When he didn't answer, she decided to let it drop.

"Mr. Lorenzo made his first fifteen-hundred-dollar payoff to you after the pre-challenge dinner, right?" she said.

Dennis confirmed her guess with a nod.

She thought back, trying to pull all the pieces of the puzzle together. "Is that when he handed over the answers to the Clues Challenge?" she asked. "You *were* the one who sent the computer threat about the clues, right?"

"Bravo," Dennis said in a sarcastic voice that rubbed Nancy the wrong way. "Ten points for the amateur detective."

Glancing up, Nancy saw George and Ned watching their progress closely from the roof. Just a little farther, and she and Dennis would be there.

"There's still something I don't get," Nancy said, turning back to Dennis. "If Mr. Lorenzo gave you the answers to the clues, why did you sabotage our team?"

"Call it extra insurance," he said, giving a shrug that seemed to say it was no big deal.

Nancy couldn't believe how callous he seemed. "C.J. sprained his ankle because of you!" she said.

"Pops is the one who rubbed the stair with soap," Dennis corrected. "At my instructions, of course. Anyway, C.J. deserved it, after the way he stole Dede from me."

"No one deserves to be hurt like that," Nancy shot back. "What about the rest of us? George's skis? The tree branch that broke while I was climbing the oak?"

"Mel did a pretty good job setting up both of those accidents," Dennis said. "I knew you suspected me, so I had him do it."

As he talked, a light blinked on inside Nancy's head. "And you set up Joy to take the blame!" she realized. "You must have planted her glove and that file on the roof of the administration building." Thinking about it made her cheeks burn. "I *knew* someone else was in the building. It was you!"

"Right again," Dennis said. "I had a feeling you'd come running after I knocked the icicle off the roof. When I saw Joy using the phone, I knew I had the perfect way to throw suspicion off myself. She didn't even hear me take her glove. And I knew you already suspected her."

"You had it all figured out, huh?" Nancy said, shaking her head in disgust.

Dennis grinned. "I made sure the Sigmas got a slow start, so we wouldn't be suspected," he bragged. "I was all set to make a stunning, come-from-behind victory." He frowned, pressing his mouth into a tight line. "Until *you* showed up."

Nancy was glad to see that they were finally at the top of the fire escape. Just above, Ned and George were dark silhouettes against the bright sun.

"You guys made it," Ned said. "We were afraid the whole thing might fall."

Nancy shuddered at the thought. "Give us a hand up, all right?" she said. "Dennis, you go fir . . ."

Her voice trailed off as a third silhouette appeared on the roof, right behind Ned and George. Nancy couldn't see the face clearly, but she didn't need to. There was no mistaking that bulky frame.

"Mr. Lorenzo!" she said.

Ned and George whirled around—then froze when they saw the huge metal wrench in Mr. Lorenzo's hand.

"Nobody moves!" Mr. Lorenzo said, waving the wrench in a threatening arc.

"Boy, am I glad to see you!" Dennis said. He reached up his hands. "Help me up, Pops. We've got to get out of here before the police come."

Mr. Lorenzo shook his head. "You've become too expensive, Dennis," he said in a frigid voice that made Nancy shiver. "You'll have to go with everyone else."

"G-go?" George echoed. "What do you mean?"

"I'm not about to let a couple of kids send me to jail—or make me go broke," he scoffed. "That's why you're all about to suffer a tragic fall from this dangerous old fire escape."

16

A Desperate Plan

"You can't!" Nancy gulped, glancing down at the snow-covered ground five stories below.

"Oh, yeah? Watch me," Mr. Lorenzo said. He turned to Ned and George. "Get down there with your friends," he ordered.

George glanced helplessly at Nancy, then began to climb over the side. Mr. Lorenzo kept a close watch on her.

"Randy went to call the police," Ned said. "They'll be here any minute." He took a step forward, then jumped back when Mr. Lorenzo swung the wrench in his direction.

"I'll be gone by then," Mr. Lorenzo said. "You kids should have kept your noses out of my business. You and that reporter."

Nancy grabbed the brick wall as George dropped onto the fire escape next to her and Dennis. "You belong in jail, Mr. Lorenzo. Or maybe I should call you Mr. Papazian."

The store owner's eyes blazed red. "So you figured it out," he said. "I thought so. It's a good thing I decided to follow you after you left the Sports Complex."

He jerked his head toward Ned. "Now you. Down with your friends," he instructed.

Ned crouched down at the edge of the roof. Nancy saw his eyes flicker briefly toward the vents at the center of the roof.

"We actually believed you when you said you liked to support college athletes," Ned said, shaking his head in disgust. "The only thing you care about is yourself."

Ned looked carefully at Nancy, meeting her gaze. Then he let his eyes flicker behind Mr. Lorenzo again. He was trying to tell her something, she was sure of it.

"Mr. Lorenzo?" Joy's voice came from somewhere on the roof. "What are *you* doing up here?"

Mr. Lorenzo turned, scowling, to look behind him. In that second, Nancy jumped into action.

"Get him!" she shouted.

Ned launched himself toward Mr. Lorenzo, catching him in a tackle that sent the big man flying face-first onto the snowy roof.

Using the rusted fire escape railing for footing, Nancy hoisted herself up onto the roof. She saw Mr. Lorenzo twist out of Ned's grasp and reach for the heavy wrench, which had dropped into the snow beside him.

"No!" she cried, vaulting forward. She reached the wrench a split-second before he did. Nancy kicked it as hard as she could, sending it skittering across the snowy rooftop. The heavy wrench stopped just a few feet from where Joy stood watching, her eyes wide with shock.

By the time Nancy turned around again, Ned and Dennis had Mr. Lorenzo pinned to the ground with his arms behind his back.

"The police are here!" George announced.

"Wh-what's going on?" Joy asked.

Looking down from the rooftop, Nancy saw a black-and-white squad car pull to a stop on the road. Randy's Jeep was right behind it. Joy's sorority sisters stood on the snowy ground, looking curiously from the police car to the rooftop of the old theater building.

"It's a long story," Nancy said. "And before we tell it, there's something I have to do."

She strode over to the wooden crate where Dennis had been when she found him. Opening the top, she reached inside and pulled out the blue-and-white Clues Challenge banner.

She held up the banner, letting it flutter in the cold winter wind. "There's a new Clues Challenge winner," she announced. "Omega Chi Epsilon!"

✧   ✧   ✧

148

"I still can't believe Grant and I were stuck scaling the wrong theater building while you guys saw all the action," C.J. said that evening.

Nancy grinned down the long table at the Eatery where she, Ned, George, C.J., Grant, and Dede sat. The rest of Dede's sorority sisters, as well as everyone from the Delta Tau and Sigma Pi teams, were also there.

The only ones missing were Dennis and Mr. Lorenzo.

"I still can't believe Mr. Lorenzo was on the run from the police for three years," Dede said. "And that Dennis was blackmailing him."

"We're still in shock about that," said Philip, leaning over from the table where he sat with the other guys from Sigma Pi. "I mean, Dennis was our friend."

Philip's brother, Jake, shook his head slowly back and forth. "We should have known something was up when Dennis bought that new computer. I knew it cost a bundle, but I never figured he got the money from blackmailing someone."

"Dennis and Mr. Lorenzo had a lot of people fooled," Nancy said. She leaned back in her chair, looking out over the platters of pasta, chicken, and grilled fish on their table. "The important thing is that they're both in jail now, where they won't be able to hurt anyone else."

Joy stood up at her table and clinked her glass with

a spoon. "I'd like to make a toast," she said. "Here's to the new Clues Challenge champs."

Nancy cheered along with everyone else.

"Of course, next year will be a different story," Joy went on when the noise died down. She grinned at her teammates. "Right?"

"Absolutely," Krista spoke up from her table. "Next year the Kappas are going to win!"

Taunts and challenges flew from table to table, but Nancy didn't join in. Leaning close to Ned, she gazed into his warm brown eyes.

"We just solved a three-year-old mystery and got two criminals off the street," she said. "I think that makes us all winners."

Do your younger brothers and sisters want to read books like yours?

Let them know there are books just for *them!*

They can join Nancy Drew and her best friends as they collect clues and solve mysteries in

THE

NANCY DREW

NOTEBOOKS®

Starting with

#1 The Slumber Party Secret

#2 The Lost Locket

#3 The Secret Santa

#4 Bad Day for Ballet

AND

Meet up with suspense and mystery in The Hardy Boys® are: The Clues Brothers™

Starting with

#1 The Gross Ghost Mystery

#2 The Karate Clue

#3 First Day, Worst Day

#4 Jump Shot Detectives

A MINSTREL® BOOK

Published by Pocket Books

2324